THE FOREST OF APP

Gloria Rand Dank

The Forest of App

GREENWILLOW BOOKS
NEW YORK

Library of Congress Cataloging in Publication Data
Dank, Gloria.   The Forest of App.
Summary: A crippled boy named Nob, left
behind by his own people, a race of storytellers,
is taken in by a witch-girl, an elf, and
a dwarf, creatures of an ancient forest from
which the magic has all but disappeared.
[1. Fantasy]   I. Title.
PZ7.D226Fo   1983   [Fic]   83-1627
ISBN 0-688-02315-0

To Leif and my family,
with love.

O N E

HE WAS SMALL AND GOLDEN. THE AMBER
light glittered on her skin as she moved
through the trees. With her, in the broken-down shack, lived Stout and Needle
and Hopeless, the dog. The first frost dancing on the
branches brought Rasp, the droll-teller, singing to their
door, and the spring wind blew in the ravens, Kay's
people, tumbling and shouting, their hoarse cries fill-
ing the air. So she never lacked for company. She and
the others had learned long ago to hide themselves
from interfering eyes. It was rare enough that strang-
ers came to the forest, but when they did, she and
Needle and the rest were nowhere to be seen.

The trees had been disturbed for a while. Soft whispers flew through their branches, murmurs of distress.
They tried to confide in the witch-brat, but she was

busy and would not listen. At last, annoyed by their entreaties, she let herself be led through the forest. The dog, Hopeless, followed behind, snuffling through the grass, small and gray and quiet.

She stopped once or twice to play, trying to turn a mouse into a wolf, fumbling with her spells, but each time the trees murmured to her, urging her on. She was about to give up and turn back when, worming her way through a thick patch of brackleberries, stopping now and then to disengage her long olive-brown hair from the eager thorns, she suddenly came upon a body lying in a clearing.

She stopped, her hands waving before her, as if to brush away the sight. Behind her the dog panted, struggling through the narrow space. He paused, stuck halfway through, and lifted his head.

There was a muffled yelp, and the dog and girl struggled to get away, the girl pushing Hopeless like a cork, backward through the groaning branches, and then scrambling after him, away, away from that body and the deathly stillness around it. It looked like a boy, his body thin and starved, lying curled like a snail in the grass.

"You should not have run away," remarked Needle disapprovingly as he served out the evening meal.

There was a silence. Hopeless mumbled to himself, hiccuping gently over his food bowl.

"Twelve," Needle rapped out, "did you hear me? I *said*, you should not have run away."

The witch-brat looked sullen. Her thin face, yellow as sand under the moon, was drawn into a frown. "He was a stranger," she replied, holding out her bowl to be filled. "He looked dead anyway," she added.

"He might be," said Needle, "and then again he might not."

Stout, at the head of the table, shook his head, his short legs dangling far above the floor. "It's not right," he said. "Not right, do you hear, Twelve? Don't you know any better?"

"Oh, leave me alone!" shrieked the girl. "Leave me alone! I wish I had never told you!"

She slammed her fist down on the table. Stout and Needle grabbed in vain for the pot as it tipped, sloshing its contents onto the wooden floor. Stout cursed, his hands covered with burning gruel. The witch wilted and shrank back in her chair.

Needle murmured something under his breath and went to fetch a cloth. "I hope this will be quite enough," he said as he mopped up the mess. "Quite enough theatrics for one day. Stout, are you all right?"

The dwarf did not reply. Glaring at Twelve, he sat back and lit his pipe. Under the table Hopeless stirred and rumbled querulously.

Needle served the food into the wooden bowls and sat down, stretching out his long, spidery legs underneath the table. Hopeless bumped his head against Twelve's knees and tried to purr; then he sprawled awkwardly in front of the fire and fell asleep, his spiky mud-gray fur outlined in sunrise against the flames.

When the meal was done, Needle sighed, pushed his chair back, and spread his thin fingers out over the table. "Now," he said, looking at his two companions, "what do we do next?"

The moon shone in wavering patches through the branches. Three figures made their way toward the edge of the forest. Twelve wore a long gray-green cloak and caressed the rough barks of the trees with her fingertips as she passed. Behind her walked Stout, probing his way through the brambles with his cane. Last of all came Needle, thin and fragile as a twig, his elfin eyes catching the moon in bursts of green light. They had left Hopeless behind to guard their home, although they knew that as soon as they left, the old dog swayed from his post at the door and collapsed again by the fire.

They walked for a long time, as the moon bubbled up into the sky. The trees whispered to Twelve when she passed and kept her on the right path. She swept by, her cloak billowing, and they questioned her about the stranger she had seen. *"Who was he?"* they murmured. *"Whoooo? Whoooooooo wassssssssssss hhhhhhhhhhhhhhhheeeeeeeeeeeeeeeeee?"*

"I don't know," said Twelve. "I don't know. We're going to find out."

Behind her Stout plodded onward, muttering to himself as the branches whipped back into his face. "Should've waited until morning," he mumbled.

"*Hsssh!*" said the reedy figure behind him. "Be quiet, both of you. We're almost there."

They fell silent. Around them the forest, too, grew still, as if pausing to listen, wood sap and leaf rustle halted for a moment.

"That's where I found it," whispered Twelve, pointing to a clump of bushes.

They reached the bushes and clustered together.

"Do—do you see anything?" said the elf.

Overhead the moon dipped and soared, casting shadows. The strange changing shapes seemed to drift like ghosts beneath the trees.

At last the dwarf lost his patience. "Enough of this," he said irritably, and stamping his walking stick on the ground, he cried, "*Who's there? Come out and show yourself!*"

"*Stout,*" whispered the elf, but the dwarf would not listen.

"Is there anyone there?" he shouted, poking about in the bushes. "*Anyone?*"

The trees heaved and sighed as he beat their sides with his stick. They trembled, sending signals to their fellows miles away, information passing swiftly and surely through the air and under the ground, flowing through the great knowing linkages of branches and roots.

"Perhaps he's moved," said Needle, and so they pushed on through the darkness, led by the trees. Soon they came to another clearing. In the center, on a hillock, sat the boy.

His face was milky pale, his hair long, curly, and unkempt, and his eyes were filled with shadows. He raised his head and gazed toward them.

Needle leaned forward. "Follow me," he whispered.

It was difficult to get through the trees. Stout grumbled and cursed as he struggled through the protesting foliage. Twelve beat her fists angrily against a knotted trunk. Needle slipped through calmly and reached the boy first.

They stared at each other.

Stout stumbled out into the open space. Twelve appeared, gasping, her face scratched.

For a long moment no one spoke. Then the boy got to his feet with a strange listing motion. "Don't come any nearer," he said.

The three forest creatures drew together at the sound of his voice. "Boy," Needle said, "what are you doing here in our forest?"

The stranger swayed. "Don't come near me," he said. "I know what you are. You're dreams . . . illusions. Leave me alone. Go away."

"What should we do?" asked the dwarf, his voice low.

"I don't know," Needle said. "It's been a long time since I've seen one of these. How old do you think it is?"

"Old enough to know better," said the dwarf. He stepped forward, his shadow lurching along in his wake, and gestured to the boy. "Go away," he said. "You don't belong here. Go away."

The boy grinned at him and did not reply.

The dwarf drew back. "Perhaps it's insane," he said to Needle. "Just look at it, the way it smiles. It might be dangerous. What should we do?"

The elf reflected.

"Let's kill it," prompted the witch in her high, childish voice.

"*Twelve!*" said Needle.

"Let's lead it out of the forest and leave it for someone else to find," suggested Stout.

The boy lifted one arm and pointed at them. "You three," he said, "don't exist." His arm dropped. He wavered and sat down heavily.

"It's mad," Stout said.

"It's just starved," said Needle. "Look at it. It hasn't had anything to eat for days probably. No one in the forest would help it."

"Then why should *we*?" asked the witch-brat.

The stranger suddenly laughed. Overhead some bats

chittered and swooped, frightened by the sound. *"Whyshouldweshouldwe?"* the boy cried, jumbling the words. His eyes swam in his head.

"Yes, well," said the elf, "perhaps it *is* a bit feeble-minded. But that is just one more reason to do something."

Stout sighed. "Should we take it back with us?" he asked.

Needle nodded.

The witch made an unpleasant sound. "No. Too much trouble. Leave it here."

The dwarf tapped his walking stick on the ground. "We'll take it back," he said, "but it *mustn't* know where we live. These humans are nosy, prying creatures. It might return and bring others with it."

The elf nodded. On his mound the boy looked up. "Are you still here?" he said. "Go away, do you hear me? Go away!" He lifted a hand to his forehead. The clearing seemed to shift, changing shape, glowing with strange colors, streaming past his bewildered eyes.

Suddenly a voice spoke to him from nearby. "Listen," it said from somewhere above him. "You'll come with me. We'll take care of you. Can you hear me?"

The boy muttered something, turning his head away.

"Can you understand me?" asked the voice again. "We'll take care of you. Will you come?"

The boy stared upward; then he staggered to his

feet. "No!" he cried. "No! I don't need any help!" And turning, he began to shuffle out of the clearing.

Striding forward, Needle swept the boy off his feet and swung him up on one shoulder. The boy smiled weakly, hanging upside down like a bag.

"Come!" said Needle to the others.

The trees drew their branches back before them.

T W O

E HAD ALWAYS BEEN CALLED THE FOOL. Ever since his parents had died and he had been taken in by his aunt Lace, added to her own large brood, the other rhymer children had tormented him for the way he looked and the way he walked. The sickness which had come and taken his parents with it had left him, as an infant, scarred and stunted, and now, although all the marks had disappeared, one of his legs was shorter than the other. It was not too bad; he could still run on it, limping. But the children teased him. It was always "Nob the cripple! Nob the fool!" At first he had met their insults with shy smiles and a gesture of entreaty, but he had quickly learned not to smile or beg. Still, in all the years of waiting, it had never occurred to him alderman and his list, and he did not seem to know where he was.

Laren sighed. "Out of my way, Nob," she said. "Move. The listing is over."

The boy twitched; then he looked at her, shyly, dully, like an animal. He put out a hand, and she saw that his eyes were filled with tears. "Look!" she shrieked. "Nob—Nob is crying! The fool is crying! He thought he was going to join the Storyfind!"

The rhymers turned back and clustered around. The children, older ones and young ones alike, began to jeer at him.

Nob drew back, his hands fluttering in the air; then he turned and limped off down the street as quickly as he could go.

"Never mind, Nob," said his aunt. "You'll stay here with me and the little ones."

"I don't want to," said the boy, suddenly fierce.

"*Tch, tch, tch,*" said Aunt Lace cheerfully. "You'll find as good a tale here as anywhere."

A week passed, and then another. The rhymers gathered in the middle of the dusty road and saw their children off, with much anxious clucking and scolding.

"Good-bye!" cried the young ones, waving, and "Good-bye!" echoed their parents and aunts and uncles and friends. The children set off in a buzzing group on the road out of town. They would scatter once they had gotten far enough away, each to pursue his or her story alone. The rhymers shouted and waved. Even an ancient hobo, leaning on an equally ancient stick by the side of the road, looked up and waved an empty wine bottle. The flies sang like a scourge around the people's eyes and ears and mouths.

Nob stood on the doorstep, watching the other children go. He waited, rubbing the dust from his eyes. Then he went inside and picked up an old brown sack. No one was in the cottage; Aunt Lace and her brood were seeing the others off. The boy limped outside, clutching the bag, his eyes on the small group of children far down the road. With a determined step he set out after them.

At first no one noticed, but all at once someone clutched Aunt Lace's arm and whispered to her, "Look! Isn't that Nob?"

His aunt turned.

The whispers spread, rippling over the crowd.

"Look! Look! It's the fool!"

"What's he doing?"

"He's going with the others!"

"He can't! He can't take care of himself! Bring him back! Bring him back!"

But no one moved. They stood watching, vaguely ashamed, as Nob limped off eagerly down the road.

T H R E E

HE DAY BROKE WIDE OPEN, LIKE AN EGG. The sun filtered gently through the trees, dapple spots slipping over the ground, gathering in a small pool in front of the door.

Inside the ramshackle cottage Needle opened his eyes. Rising to his feet, he shook his head to clear the dreams away and staggered outside, yawning, to get water for the kettle.

In the gray-green darkness behind the door Stout turned on his pallet and muttered to himself. Hopeless spread his mouth in a great drooling yawn. Twelve opened her eyes, suddenly and fully awake, in witch fashion, and narrowed her dark gaze on the sleeping boy.

Nob lay on a mat, one arm thrown behind his head,

his face twitching with unforgiving dreams. His body was thin; he looked drawn and fragile. They had found his small bag of belongings lying beside the mound and had taken it back with them. It rested next to his head.

The witch glared in distaste. He looked about her age. She turned, and in a low voice she called, "Hopeless! Hopeless, come here!"

The old dog grumbled in his sleep, his tail wagging feebly.

"Hopeless!" whispered Twelve, and the gray shape rose, to shuffle across the room and collapse in a whirlwind of dust next to her bed.

The dog sighed and went back to sleep. The witch buried her hands in his moth-bitten fur and whispered to herself angrily. Stout was snoring on his bed, and Needle was outside. Twelve looked around. She rose to her feet, and gliding across the floor, she stopped next to the sleeping boy. She looked around once again. Then she kicked him, hard, in the ribs.

Nob groaned and flinched. He started to get up. The witch kicked him again.

A long-legged shape came flying through the air, and Twelve was lifted in Needle's clutches and borne, shrieking, outside. Stout was on his feet, blinking like a mole and mumbling, "Whazzat?" before he saw the boy with a hand to his side, groaning. The dwarf knelt and examined Nob's bruises. "Not too bad," he muttered. The elf came back in, his face set and grim.

The witch-child followed, her eyes bright with tears, the dog at her side. She went to the table and sat down, crossing her hands primly on her lap.

"The boy is a guest in our house," announced Needle, "and will be treated as such. No spites, no petty jealousies. Do you hear me, Twelve?"

"Yes," said the witch, grinning at him savagely.

"Don't think I don't know what that means," he replied. "But you won't get a second chance at him. I'll have my eye on you from now on."

Nob looked up at him, taking in the narrow face, shadowed with deep lines and crevasses; the dark thatch of hair; and the leaf-green eyes, kindly, with a distant expression. "Time for breakfast," Needle said.

They gave Nob soup and bread, which he finished off, holding his bowl out for more. At his side the witch ate decorously, breaking her biscuit into careful squares, neatly decapitating a piece of fruit and carving it into cubes. She fed some bread to Hopeless under the table. Whenever Needle glanced at her, she smiled back at him sweetly.

After breakfast the boy was led back to his mat, where he slipped into the sleep of exhaustion. When he awoke again, it was night, and Needle and Stout were sitting in their chairs by the empty fireplace, reading by the light of thick wax candles. The smell of smoke was heavy in the air, from the guttering candles and from the dwarf's pipe, which he drew on fiercely. Needle's eyes were watering from the acrid smoke.

"For God's sake, Stout, could you please take your pipe outside?" he asked irritably.

Muttering, the dwarf stood up, and taking a candle from the table, he stomped out the door, his book under his arm.

Nob sat up.

"So you're awake," said the elf.

Nob stared at him. The elf gazed back, unblinking. "It's rude to stare," Needle admonished mildly. He returned to his book.

Nob glanced around the small room, with its fireplace, its rickety table and chairs, and the two larger chairs which Stout and Needle used for reading. The room had a used look, a look of decay.

The boy's memories of the past few days were faint, jumbled, snatches here and there, a face bent over him in concern, a voice . . . he shook his head. He remembered going into the forest to find food; he remembered wandering, lost, hungry, the trees themselves seeming to play tricks, paths opening and closing, vanishing before him.

Stout came back into the room and gave the boy a quick glance. "Hungry?"

Nob nodded.

When he finished eating, he sat at the table uncertainly. Stout and Needle both were deep in their books. After giving him food, they had not bothered to talk to him.

"Don't—don't you want to know who I am?" he said at last.

"No," Needle said.

There was a long pause. Stout pulled on the stem of his unlit pipe noisily.

"My name is Nob," the boy said, then added, flushing, "The fool. Nob the fool."

There was no reply. Needle turned a page.

Nob looked down at his plate. He fumbled with his fork and spoon. "Who—who are you?"

The elf glanced up. "I am called Needle, and this is Stout."

"What are you going to do with me?" Nob asked.

"Well," Needle said, staring at the cold logs in the hearth, "I'm not sure yet. You shouldn't have come here in the first place, you know."

Nob nodded. He looked down at the smooth wood of the tabletop. He blinked, and suddenly the room swam, and he staggered to his feet.

"I'm the fool," he said. "Nob the fool! The others— the others got to go, but they wouldn't let me . . . they wouldn't let me. But I went! I went anyway. And I got lost . . . I was afraid to go into the towns . . . I knew they'd laugh . . . they'd laugh at me!"

He swayed on his feet.

"I told you," said the dwarf, "that he was feeble-minded."

"No," said Needle, coming forward. "He's just exhausted, that's all."

He led the boy gently back to the sleeping mat. The last thing Nob remembered, before he fell asleep, was the sight of Needle's face bent over him.

The rhymers had often told tales of strange creatures in the forest, faces glimpsed peering from the bushes, a snatch of song heard late at night. Many villagers accepted these stories as true, and hunting parties took care to skirt the old forest near the town of App. The tales were told and retold. Aunt Lace often entertained her children with stories of unicorns, goblins, and elves. She had always wanted to see a unicorn, she said, even if it was only a quick glimpse from afar. Nob had listened, curled up at her side.

"I suppose we'll have to keep him," said Needle, "for a while."

Twelve chewed her lip, pouting, while next to her Stout sucked on his pipe and stared at the ground. They were seated under a tree in the small clearing outside their home. Across from them, his face hidden in the shade cast by an oak, Nob was sprawled on his back, his arms crossed behind his head.

"I don't like it," said Stout, his voice low. "It was right to rescue him and all that, but this is going too far. There's been a lot of talk, you know, Needle."

"There's always a lot of talk," the thin figure said composedly. "The forest chatters about a leaf falling. That's not our concern."

"Nonetheless," said the dwarf, "nonetheless. It's a warning. It's not a good sign, they say. He doesn't belong here. The forest is afraid of more bad luck."

"More?" said Needle. "It couldn't have any more."

Twelve looked from one to the other. The dwarf was hunched inside himself, his shoulders bowed, while Needle sat calmly, plaiting twigs and grass together to form a basket. It was three days since they had found Nob, and the clean, neat-edged shape of their lives had been disrupted. Even their daily routine had been thrown off by the boy's presence: They still went dutifully about their tasks; but their thoughts were elsewhere, and their motions were slow, doubtful, like an old wheel turning. Hopeless seemed permanently confused by Nob. He stared at the boy from across the room, his hair prickling in all directions; he would no longer come to the table to sit under Twelve's feet and beg for scraps. He bowed his head and growled, a pathetic attempt at menace whenever Nob came near.

"He says it shouldn't be very long before his people return," Needle said soothingly.

Nob had been wandering on his Storyfind for weeks, seeking stories here and there, haunting the edges of towns, plodding along the road, until finally, in desperation, he had plunged into the forest in search of food. He knew that it was long past time for the rhymers to move on. The Storyfind was supposed to last a week, or perhaps two; but in that time no tale had found him, and so he went on stubbornly, sniffing at the outskirts of towns like a dog. He knew that the others who had gone on Storyfind would already have returned, and he knew, painfully, that his people would not wait for him. His aunt would beg them to stay; but they would assume him lost or dead or run off, and they would have a schedule to meet, performances to play in the next town. The rhymers followed a different route every year, so there was no telling where they would go next; but Nob was sure that sooner or later they would turn back toward the forest, wending their way south, perhaps stopping to play in Ague or Mud or Rinaldan.

"I'll send out the ravens to spy on the nearby villages," said Needle. "They'll tell us when the rhymers return."

"If we can trust Kay and his thieves to tell us what they see," said the dwarf sourly.

Twelve said nothing. She sat, her olive hair streaming around her. Her hand absently stroked Hopeless's back. The dog raised his head and regarded her lovingly, his eyes blue and filmy with the years.

"It's time," said Needle, "to pay a visit to Granny Weil."

From behind a large pile of clothes on the table, where he was busy mending and darning, Stout groaned. "Not again, so soon!" he cried.

"I'm afraid so," said the elf, making up a bundle of food. "It seems no one else will go."

"Well, what are we going to do with *him*?" asked Stout, indicating the boy, who looked up from his seat near the window.

"Why don't we take him along?" Needle suggested. "Granny might like to meet him."

Twelve grinned. "Granny," she said, "doesn't like to meet *anybody*."

"Take your jacket," Needle said to Nob. "It's cold out."

They left, locking the door and turning their faces to the brisk wind. All around them the forest was deepening into gold and plum and gentle lavender. Hopeless stayed behind by the fire.

Granny Weil's dwelling was an hour's walk away. She lived near the center of the forest, in a deep cave carved from the side of a hillock, with crumbling earth above and below. They came, the four of them, and stood at the opening.

Needle cleared his throat. "Granny?" he called. "Granny? Granny Weil?"

There was no response.

Needle shifted from one foot to the other. "Granny?" he shouted, and the crumbling walls echoed with his voice, crying, *"Granny? . . . Granny? . . . Granny?"* into what seemed an infinite distance.

They waited, but there was nothing, no sound, no movement from within.

Twelve giggled. "She's playing her tricks again," she muttered.

"Sssshhh!" said Needle.

"What tricks?" whispered Nob. "Who is she?"

"Stay back," counseled Stout. "Don't go too close. You never know when she'll come out."

There was silence. Once more Needle leaned forward and shouted into the darkness, *"Granny! Granny Weil! We're here! We—we've come to pay you a visit!"*

There was no answer, no answer, but all at once a portion of the darkness coalesced within the cave. A small shape huddled in the distance.

"Granny?" asked Needle, straining his eyes.

They waited, and after a long silence a voice came drifting out. *"Eh?"* it asked querulously.

"There you are, Granny!" cried Needle. "May we come in?"

"Eh?" repeated the ancient voice.

"It's Needle!" shouted the elf. "Needle and Stout and Twelve! Come for a *visit*! Aren't you going to let us in, Granny?"

There was a pause.

"Go away," snapped the voice irritably, and the shape turned and vanished.

Needle fell back, muttering furiously to Stout. Twelve hovered near the entrance, peering into the cave, and Nob limped up next to her to get a better look. There was nothing to be seen except the darkness, hanging in the cave like a bat.

"Granny," coaxed Needle, bringing forth the basket of food, "look here, we've brought you lunch. Now don't you want us to come in?"

There was no reply.

"Granny," said the elf, his voice as thin as his lips, "if you don't want to invite us in, we'll just leave the basket and go away. Do you hear me?"

"He goes through this every time," whispered Stout to the boy. "The same thing, over and over."

"We'll go away, I'm telling you!" Needle was shouting now. "We'll go away, and we won't come back! Can you hear me?"

"The same thing," said Stout, "every time."

Needle threw down the basket and kicked it into the cave; then, leaning forward, he shouted a final angry farewell. He had begun to move off, the others following him, when all at once the voice said sulkily, "You've spilled it!"

Needle sighed and turned around. Stout murmured something in his ear. Nob crept back up to the entrance of the cave, his eyes wide.

The dwarf leaned forward to speak, but before he could say anything, the voice, in an entirely different tone, demanded, *"What's that?"*

"What?" cried Stout.

"That! Beside you there."

Stout glanced around him; then, grabbing Nob's arm, he shouted, "Is this who you mean, Granny?"

"Yessss." The voice sighed. "What is it?"

"It's a friend of ours, come to visit you!" called the dwarf.

There was a long, echoing pause; then: *"Is it human?"*

Stout looked at Needle. "Yes, he is," the dwarf replied.

There was a great clacking and tsking from the darkness, and the voice, high with excitement, announced, *"I shall cook it for my dinner!"*

Nob shrank back, looking wildly around him.

"I shall cook it and carve it and eat it!" cried the voice, interested at last; and far away, at the back of the cave, a candle was lit. Nob could see nothing in the small circle of light it cast, but the voice breathed, "Do come in . . . yes, come on in," ending in a wild, high cackle.

The candle began to drift away from them, into the heart of the hill.

"*No!*" cried the boy, his arms flailing, struggling as they tried to push him forward. Needle clapped a hand over his mouth and whispered, "Nothing's going to happen to you!"

Twelve laughed.

The hillock in which Granny Weil lived was shaped like a snail's shell: hollow, with a long passageway that curled around itself until it reached a central room, in the heart of the hill. They moved through the darkness, their only beacon the faint candle held by Granny Weil, which seemed to go around and around until Nob's head spun. Ahead of them the small shape spoke to itself in a continuous low voice, clacking and tsking and making horrible grinding noises with its teeth.

Finally, after many steps, the boy could see a dimly lit space ahead of them. It was a room, small and damp, with a dirt floor and dribbling threads of moss hanging from the walls. There was a cleverly constructed fireplace against one side of the room. The short, fat shape of Granny Weil, sketched sharply against the flame glow, moved into the chamber and went over to the huge caldron, as large as she was, which squatted on top of the fire. Twelve and Needle and Stout came in after her, pulling the boy along.

Granny Weil turned and grinned, displaying an

astonishing variety of broken and yellowing teeth. "Come in, come in, do," she cackled. "Come in! Don't mind the dead dog, don't mind him at all, my dears, just step around him. Do come on in!"

On the floor at their feet was sprawled a small, scrawny animal, something between a dog and a rat, which blinked up at them sleepily and, with enormous effort, opened his mouth to growl. He was splotched all over with brown and white and pink and was mainly hairless, except for a ridge of fur down his back and some broken white whiskers which stood out awkwardly from his nose. Having growled, he closed his eyes and went back to sleep.

"*Heh-heh-heh,* a dead dog," said Granny Weil, and turning away from them, she busied herself at the caldron.

Nob looked up, a frightened question in his eyes, to meet Needle's warning gaze. "It's her familiar, a spirit in the shape of a dog. He used to help her with her spells," the elf murmured. "But neither of them can do anything anymore, and she likes to pretend he's dead. He sleeps all the time now."

"*Heh-heh-heh,* my dears," said the old witch, stirring and stirring in her caldron. "*Heh-heh-heh!* Would you like some lunch?" She turned and leered at them, and Nob got his first good look at Granny Weil.

She was old, and fat, as wide as she was tall. She wore a patched many-colored dress, with a long petticoat scratching the ground at her feet and a blue ribbon tied around her waist. She had a look of clumsy softness about her, a kind of marshmallowness, which made her seem quite comfortable. But her mouth was horrible, all wrinkled and collapsed, and tiny lines crisscrossed her face and hands, like the imprint of a spider web. And her eyes were wrong somehow, not quite blue, not quite brown, more dark than light. She smiled at them now and waved a wooden spoon in the air.

"*Heh-heh-heh!*" she rattled. "*Heh-heh-heh!* Would you like some lunch, my dears?"

"That would be nice, Granny," said Needle stiffly, and he pointed toward the basket. "Just look in there, why don't you?"

"*No!*" shrieked the old woman, and spat at him. "No! None of your tasteless stuff! I know what we'll have . . . yes, I know, I know. . . ." And mumbling to herself, she bustled over to one of the shelves which lined her walls, all toppling over with vials and books and cracked dishes, and carefully selected several small dusty jars. After carrying them over to the table, she pried the first one open and held up its contents.

"Loathweed!" she announced, and flung it into the steaming caldron. The next ingredient was revealed as salamander skin, the one after that she named wolfbane, and then came mouse intestines, goat's eyes, white owl's blood. The old witch giggled and snarled as she added them to the broth.

When she was done, she whirled about, the wooden spoon held up. *"Heh-heh-heh!"* Some of the broth sloshed out of the spoon. "Soup's done! And now who will try it first, my dears? Who?"

Needle started to move forward; but Granny's eyes swept past him, and she shrieked, *"No! Stop him! Stop him!"*

Nob had slipped out of the chamber and was pelting down the passage.

In three large bounds Needle had caught up with him. Lifting the boy in his arms, the elf carried him, protesting, back into the room.

"He'll be the one to try my soup!" cried the old witch happily.

The boy fought like a demon, but Needle held him down and, stooping, said into his ear, *"It's all right, it's all right, I tell you!"*

"Now, now, my dear," whimpered the old woman, leaning over him. "Now, now, this won't hurt a bit. Just a taste of Granny's soup, there's a good boy. There's a good boy. Just a taste."

And with a shriek she pried open Nob's mouth and filled it like a cup with burning liquid.

The boy gasped, choking, his eyes streaming, but he swallowed bravely. Coughing, he glared up into Granny's eyes.

The soup was delicious.

"You see," whispered Needle. "She invents names for all the ingredients just to amuse herself."

Through all this the rat-dog had slept peacefully. Now he opened one eye and winked at Nob.

Twelve was laughing, her voice shrill.

"Is she Twelve's grandmother?" Nob asked Needle.

The elf shook his head. "She belongs to all of us," he said sadly.

From over near the fire Granny gave a sudden piercing shriek. "Here we are!" she cried, and balancing four bowls unsteadily on a tray, she shuffled over to the table. "Lunchtime! Lunchtime, my dears!"

They seated themselves on the rickety chairs and fell to. Granny stood with one old claw on Needle's shoulder, grinning at them all the while.

"That's right," they heard her say. "That's right, my dears. Eat it all up. Granny's good broth."

Now and again she would cackle, in a high whistling voice, and glance over at the dog, who never opened his eyes to look back at her.

When they were finished, she produced a strawberry pie and cut each of them a large piece. They protested that they were full, but she banged the spoon on the table until the bowls jumped. "How *dare* you!" she screeched. "How *dare* you!"

Humbly they bit into the pie, the sweet fruit bursting and rising like bubbles, a cool scarlet taste.

"That's better," snarled the witch, and her withered hand shook on Needle's shoulder.

Lunch over, she swept around the table, snatching up the dishes and piling them high in the corner, in the dust. "Wash them later," she mumbled, and seating herself at the table, on an ancient rocking chair, she smiled at them.

"Well, now, my dears," she said, "what do you have to tell me today?"

Needle and Stout and Twelve hesitated, looking at each other.

"Well, Granny," began the elf, "as you know, winter is coming, and we've been gathering food for the—"

"I don't want to talk about that!" shrieked the old woman, lifting herself half out of her chair and spitting at him viciously. There was a shocked silence, while she settled herself back into the cushions, smoothing down her raggedy dress with careful hands.

"Now, what else would you like to talk about?" she inquired.

Nob was dumbfounded. Around him the others shifted in their chairs.

It was Twelve's turn. "I don't know whether I told you this last time, Granny," she piped up, her hands straying over the table, "but the trees have been telling me *such* stories about—"

"I don't want to hear about it!" screamed the old witch,

rocking forward in her chair and slamming her hand down on the table. *"Trees!* The trees say this, the trees say that! That's all you ever have to talk about!"

Twelve fell silent, tears flashing to her eyes. She lowered her head.

They sat there, abashed, under Granny's wicked gaze, until finally Stout cleared his throat and ventured, "I heard that the last time the bogles were here, Granny, you told them that—"

"Good Lord!" snarled the old woman. "If you don't have anything to say, then *be quiet!"*

There followed a profound pause. They sat there, the four of them, their heads lowered, their eyes fixed upon the gnarled wood of the tabletop. At the head of the table the old woman rocked back and forth. "Idiots," they heard her mutter. "Idiots, all of them."

Suddenly her gaze fell on the rhymer boy. The old woman leaned forward, halting the chair's motion. It protested with a loud groan. She rested one claw on the table and then slowly smiled at Nob.

"Boy," she said, "what do you have to say to me today?"

Nob lifted his head.

"Boy," she repeated, "boy, what do you have to say to me?"

"Granny," said Needle, "I think that you—"

"Be quiet!" said the hag, turning on him. She banged the spoon on the table. "Be quiet, do you hear?" Turn-

ing back to the boy, she smiled and whispered, *"Speak to me!"*

The boy looked into her shrunken eyes, and at her worn clothes, and at her round, comfortable shape, and he thought suddenly of his aunt, small, round, and comfortable, sitting by the fire and spinning stories out of the air.

"I—I have a story I could tell," he said hesitantly.

"A story!" cried Granny Weil. "Good, good—a story! Tell me a story!" Leaning back, she rocked wildly in her chair.

Nob glanced around the table, and in a small voice he began, "This story is about—"

"Louder!" ordered Granny, pounding on the arm of the chair as it carried her back and forth. *"Louder!"*

"This story," cried Nob, "is about a witch—a witch who lived in a great dark forest."

He paused. Granny's chair went squeak, squeak . . . squeak, squeak . . . squeak, squeak into the silence.

"She was a powerful witch, very powerful, the terror of the woods in her time," the boy said slowly. "She never did any real harm; but if someone annoyed her, she would turn him into a mouse, as punishment, and then sometimes an owl would get him before she had a chance to turn him back into his proper form and she would mourn and weep for days. She often acted out of spite, for witches are very spiteful creatures, but she would always regret it afterward."

He paused. The chair had come to a stop. Granny Weil leaned forward.

Nob looked down at the table. His hands were shaking. The only audience he had ever had before was the fire and sometimes the baby Gertrude, the youngest of his aunt's children. The other children practiced by telling stories to each other, but he had had no friends, no way of knowing that his was a special gift. Still, he had always been able to take a hint here, a glance there and weave them into stories, which he told to himself.

"Yes, she would always regret it bitterly," he said. "And the creatures who were truly under her protection led charmed lives. She and—and her dog"—his eyes had fallen on the rat-dog, sprawled in his endless dreams against the wall—"would roam through the forest, casting spells, picking quarrels, turning animals into men and back again. And whenever there was a storm—oh, how they loved storms!—they would ride high and wild among the clouds, and her laughter could be heard for miles around."

He paused again.

"Go on," Granny commanded.

"She and her dog lived together in a cave—"

"A tipi," corrected Granny distantly.

"A tipi," Nob said, "a small one, with a fire in the center which sent smoke rising and curling into the sky. And there she used to make magic potions and dark liquids, and the dog would bring back small animals for her to try her evil recipes on. And she would change rats into snakes, and snakes into wolves, and wolves into deer, and deer into men, strange godlike men with antlers, who haunted the forest and countryside; and she would consort with goblins and werewolves, and when the darkness came, she would fly out of the tipi with a shriek and vanish into the moon. And yet the forest creatures loved her and feared her, and her name was a byword for power that strikes in the night. And so she lived for many, many years."

The boy stopped. So far he had guessed well, but he was young and inexperienced.

"And then," he said slowly, "the forest—the forest began to change. It began to change and decay, and everything inside it began to die."

"Not to die," said Granny, her eyes huge and frozen. "Not to die. Just to change."

"Everything began to change," said Nob, sweating and closing his eyes, "and—and one day the witch found she could no longer turn a wolf into a mouse, as hard as she tried, and the next day she could not fly within the thunder, and after that, gradually, after a long, long time, she couldn't remember even the simplest spell. Her powers went away from her, not all at once but slowly, slowly, like a picture fading. And then at the end her dog—her dog . . ." He paused, faltering.

"Her dog went to sleep," continued Granny sweetly, dreamily, "and never woke up again. And she turned against the forest, which had betrayed her . . . and she cursed the wind . . . and at last she went deep into the earth and stayed there, brewing up her broths, trying to remember. Trying to remember . . ."

"Trying to remember," murmured the dwarf, cradling his head in his hands. "But nothing was the same . . . afterward."

"No," said Needle, and he, too, bent his head.

"Nothing," murmured Twelve. "Nothing . . ."

"The dog never woke up," said Granny thickly. "He just went to sleep and went away and left her there, all alone."

There was a long silence, broken only by the crackling of the fire.

"Go away," said Granny Weil suddenly, turning from them. "Go away. I never wanted you to come. Go away."

They rose and gathered up their cloaks and whispered their good-byes, but the old witch said nothing, sitting with her face to the flames.

They hurried out into the passageway and followed it around and around till at last it threw them out into the sunlight. Blinking and rubbing their eyes, they moved down the slope, away from Granny Weil's hill.

F O U R

T FIRST IT WAS ONLY NEEDLE, LIVING BY
himself in the forest. He had stayed behind when the other elves departed,
years before. Their magic and that of the
other woodfolk had begun to fade, and the elves had
lost faith in the forest. Tales of them came from other
places, drifting back slowly, carried by the ravens or
the trees to Needle's ear. He had been joined by Stout
after the dwarf had quarreled with his people over the
ownership of a certain clump of brackleberries. Most of
the dwarfs had stayed, for magic was not in their
blood; and some goblins, and a handful of bogles,
those strange creatures, shorter and uglier than goblins, who live in burrows and eat bats; and a cluster of
naiads, those that did not swim downstream to be con-
sumed by the great white sea. And for a time the forest

had been visited by people from other places, all searching, searching: witches and wizards, elves and goblins, plus an occasional hag or two. Though they did not stay, their names and adventures came back, years later, in the shape of drolls and rhymer tales. But the creatures that stayed in the forest of App were as forgotten as driftwood after the storm.

One of those who passed through the forest left behind a girl child with brown eyes and golden skin and a knowing smile. A witch-woman had brought her to Needle one evening and had begged him to keep the girl until she came back. It was too dangerous, she said, to take the child with her. Who knows where her search might lead? Needle looked down at the witch-brat, standing sturdily in the doorway, a small brown puppy at her heels, and he looked at Stout, and they said yes. They would keep her until the witch-woman returned. They took the child in, with her dog, Hopeless, and fed them, and put up with the girl's pranks and evil ways. The years passed by, and Twelve grew strong and malicious and full of tricks. The witch-woman never came back.

After the visit to Granny Weil, Twelve treated Nob with more respect. The boy would look up to find her staring at him, solemnly, her dark eyes huge in her dust-amber face. At her side always was the gray molting pile of Hopeless, his eyes fierce under his fringe of matted hair. The old dog followed her everywhere, shambling after her as she walked, wheezing softly to himself.

Once a week Needle sent out the ravens to look for the rhymer troupe, but each time they came back with no news except some tidbits concerning the world outside and the comings and goings of men. And so the forest slipped from the colors of fall into the dead brown and white of winter, and the scarlet leaves lay thickly underfoot.

"No news," cried the ravens as they soared overhead, glossy dark against the sky, "no news!"

"Are you sure?" cried the elf, squinting up into the flat sun. "No sign of them anywhere?"

"No sign!" shrieked the ravens, spinning on the wind. "No sign! See you next week!"

Their leader, the great black raven Kay, would now and then pause in midair, his wings held stiffly aloft, and plunge downward to land on a branch above the elf's head. There he would cock a wild eye at Needle and preen himself lovingly with his dewclaw as he talked.

"What news?" the elf asked, each time, and in reply, the raven would close his eyes meditatively and stroke his feathers.

"There's a great fire burning, burning, burning, over thataway," he would say in his gravelly voice, pointing randomly with his foot, or he would smile to himself and croak, "Trouble with a thief at the crossroads." But all this had nothing to do with what Needle wanted to hear, as the raven well knew. He would grin and peer down at the elf, whose anxious face was lifted toward him; then he would hop about on the branch and shrug his wings and chuckle to himself.

"There's a tourney going on, a tourney, a great one," he'd say meanly, or, "No, no, things look quiet out there, just the usual stuff, nothing special." The elf would sigh and trudge away, back to the broken-down cottage, and the bird would screech in glee and lift his wings and be aloft in a second, streaming at the head of his tattered troops.

And so the long days withered into winter, and Needle no longer went to confer with the ravens, for wherever the boy's people were, they would not be back before spring. During the winter the rhymers put up at whatever town they were in and settled down to wait out the snow. Only when the earlypetals bloomed would they again be on the move.

So life in the cottage went on, day by day, until one morning there was a great screaming and cawing and fluttering of wings outside the door.

"Needle!" screeched a hoarse voice, rising and falling in the air. "Needle! Come out! Come out!"

The elf jumped to his feet and scurried outside, to be greeted by a fluttering and shrieking that nearly deafened him. "Enough now!" he cried, beating at the dark shapes which swept all around him. "Enough! What is it? Kay?"

"*Aaaawwwcckk!*" cried the great bird, twisting his tongue in excitement. "It's the Mester Stoorworm! The river's frozen, and the stoorworm's frozen in it! We tried to make it leave, but it's mad, mad, mad as a magpie! It won't listen to us!"

"The stoorworm?" Needle repeated stupidly, and in reply the black bird and all his companions opened their beaks and cawed.

"*Yes!*" cried Kay, and with a graceful sweep of his wing, he turned and drifted away into the air. "Yes!" he cried, his voice coming faintly with the wind. "The stoorworm! We've done what we could!"

The elf went back inside. "Stout," he said, "the Mester Stoorworm has gone and gotten itself frozen again. The ravens saw it in the river."

Stout shook his head. "Not again!"

"Come on," said Needle, gathering up blankets in his arms. "We'll have to see what we can do. I should've asked the ravens to tell the others."

"Would they listen?" asked Stout, going over to the door for his staff. "Would they help?"

"They did last time," said Twelve.

"That's no guarantee," snapped the dwarf. "Things are different now. That was a year ago."

"But the stoorworm hasn't changed," said Twelve.

"It's just gotten smaller," Needle said. He glanced at Nob.

"Let the boy come," he said in a low voice to Stout. "We'll need his help."

They left, burrowing through the snow. Hopeless stayed behind, sprawled next to the hearth, looking a bit too much like Granny's dead dog, thought the boy as he shrugged himself into a winter jacket of Needle's and ran from the house with the others.

They trudged for what seemed like hours through the black corpses of the trees, standing stiffly with their roots buried in snow. It was winter, and the forest was asleep, dreaming frozen dreams. As she went past, the witch still touched the scaly barks of the trees and murmured to them, but there was no reply. The trees were too sluggish, their sap running slowly, to rouse themselves for her.

Finally they came upon an ice-blue river and followed it for a while, stumbling in the snowdrifts on its banks. Nob was lagging behind, limping badly, groaning to himself, when at last they came upon a bend in the river where the waters widened to form a small pond.

"There it is," said Needle, and they lifted their heads to stare across the plate of ice.

In the center of the pond a large rock rose grandly

from the water: a rock which was laced and trellised with layer after layer of terraces, like an ancient castle or a miniature mountain. It was iron-gray and wore a cap of snow jauntily, at a tilt. Around its base, coiled in loop after thick loop on a tiny island of pebbles and shards, lay a serpent, gray as stone, also with a cap of snow. Its blunt head was up, swaying, questing about, eyes glittering. From the bottom of its jaw dripped a stalactite, large as a fang. The four of them huddled at the edge of the trapped waters. Nob gazed in awe at the snake, which did not seem to see them.

"Well, there it is," muttered the dwarf, shifting his blankets from one arm to the other. "There it is. What now?"

"Let's try to be friendly," said Needle. "Let's try talking to it."

"It'll do no good," said Stout, but he moved aside to let Needle come up to the edge of the lake.

"Hail, Mester Stoorworm!" Needle cried. "Hail and well met!"

The snake's head shot up about two feet. It stared across the water at them blindly. "Hail!" it cried, its voice thin and eager in the icy air. "Hail! Who is it? Who goes there?"

"It's Needle and Stout and Twelve!" shouted the elf. "We've come to see how you are, Mester!"

The blunt head drifted in the air, and the flat forked tongue quivered in and out. "How am I?" the creature cried happily. "How am I? I'm well, thank you! Very well! And you?"

"Very well, thank you!" shouted Needle.

At his side Stout stamped his feet into the snow and growled, "Come on, get to the point!"

"Good, good!" replied the serpent in its delicate, raspy voice. Its tongue flickered joyously. "Good! Thank you so much for coming to visit! See you next year!"

"No!" cried Needle, "no!" But it was too late: The serpent had turned away from them and slithered, coil sliding over glossy coil, around to the other side of the rock. From there they could hear it talking rapidly to nothing.

Needle turned and sighed, and next to him, Stout snapped, "That was excellent. Excellent. So what do we do now?"

"It won't leave the pond," Needle said to the boy. "For years now, it hasn't had the sense to go someplace warm and hibernate until spring."

"We'd better do something," Stout said. "Or it'll get stuck to the ice on that rock."

Needle handed his pile of blankets to the boy, and Stout gave his to Twelve.

"Follow us," said the elf. "Don't say anything. Just be ready with these when we tell you. And watch your step—the ice is dangerous."

They set off across the frozen pond, stepping carefully, like blind men: first Needle, creeping across the water like a huge insect; then Stout, his walking stick testing for weak spots; and finally Nob and Twelve, their arms piled high with blankets.

As they approached the rock, the snake's head appeared again, slightly tilted, listening, and the creature coiled quickly around to face them. As they got nearer, Nob could see that its eyes were reddish green and tiny. It squinted nearsightedly toward the sound of their footsteps. Its small, fogged eyes ran confusedly over the ice.

As they drew near, it paused, its head held rigid, and then withdrew swiftly into its coils and pressed against the rock and said in a deep, hissing voice, "Halt! *Halt*, I say! Who goes there?"

Needle paused a few feet away. "It's us, stoorworm," he said. "Just us. Needle and Stout and Twelve. Your friends."

The snake glared. Its icecap was slipping over its face. "What? Friends?" it demanded hoarsely. "I have no friends." Its body, shingled with iron-gray scales, writhed against the stone. It opened its glowing red mouth and hissed. From this close the boy could see that its thick loops were covered with driblets of ice, small icicles that clung to its sides and made a silvery sound when it moved. Its tail was looped around a stone, then trailed off miserably, held fast in the ice.

"Now, now, Mester Stoorworm," Needle was saying, "now, now, you don't mean that, do you? Of course, you have friends. We are your friends. We have come to help you."

"Help?" the serpent demanded in a small, mean voice. *"Help?* The Mester Stoorworm needs no help. The Mester Stoorworm has only to open its mouth and breathe out, and its fiery breath will ravage the world. The Mester Stoorworm has only to reach out with its giant tongue to sweep entire villages and mountains into the sea. The Mester Stoorworm has only to tighten its great coils around the largest ship to burst it like an egg." It spat. "Now tell me, mortal: What *help* does the Mester Stoorworm need?"

Needle and Stout shifted, glancing at each other.

The snake peered at them, its voice low, suddenly dispirited. "The Mester is the first of the great stoorworms," it said. "Do you hear? The first, the greatest, and the largest of all the stoorworms. And I—*I* am the Mester Stoorworm."

"Of course," said Needle.

"I was the first," cried the serpent, and its head reared up. "The first! Here is my mountain, and here is the sea! Tell me, mortal, how is it that you came here? How did you find me? Where is your ship?"

Needle sighed. "I left my ship over yonder," he said, pointing, and the snake's gaze slid along his finger and searched the far shore eagerly. "We came to seek the great Mester, the first of all the stoorworms.

We came to find you here, in this vast ocean, astride this great rock."

"*Aaaaaaahhhhhhhh,*" sighed the serpent. "*Aaaaaaa-hhhhhhhh.*" Its head dropped low, and its eyes gazed lovingly into Needle's. "Yeeessssss. This great rock. I sssseee."

"Mester," said Needle, "struck with awe as we are before your grandeur, I must tell you that we have come to take you back with us. The ocean is no longer safe for one such as you."

"What?" cried the snake, and its nose shot up. "*What?* The ocean no longer welcomes me? You lie! You lie!" It sank lower and stared around at the blue pond, its breath hissing through its fangs. The stalactite on its chin quivered. "It's not true!"

"Mester," said Needle, taking a cautious step backward, "I regret to tell you that it is true. We have come all this way on our ship to find you and tell you this. You must leave your mountain now and come with us. We will guard you safely until the ocean is calm again."

"Noooooooooo," said the snake in an ugly tone. "Nnnooooo. Never. Never will I leave the sea."

"Mester," said the elf, "you must. You must come with us. If you stay here, you will die."

"Then let me die!" cried the snake wildly, rearing into the frostbitten air and making frantic lunges all around. "Then let me die, I say! I would rather die here on my mountain than live to be carried away, like a piece of wood!"

"All right!" stormed the dwarf. "All right then! Stay here, you wretched thing—stay here, with your rock and your little pond! See if we care! We'll just go away and let you freeze to death!"

Needle grabbed Stout's arm. The serpent turned its head in Stout's direction and gazed at him vaguely. *"Pond?"* they heard it murmur.

"Yes, pond!" shouted the dwarf. "Pond, and wretched rock, and it's winter, you fool! The water's frozen over, and soon you would be, too, if it weren't for us!"

"Winter?" the snake said stupidly to itself.

"Winter, and my feet are freezing off!" mourned the dwarf, and stamped off in a circle around the rock.

Needle motioned to Nob and Twelve to come closer. "Mester," he said, "there's no time to waste. Stout is right. This is not the ocean, and that is not a mountain; this is a pond, and that's a rock, and it's time you came with us, without the usual trouble. We'll take you someplace warm and dry, and you'll feel better in no time."

The snake turned its unhappy gaze on him. "How dare you?" it cried, rippling up to form a great shepherd's crook against the sky. "How dare you? You'll never take me alive," it added, and sat back to watch them.

Behind Needle, the witch stooped down and laid her blankets on the ice. "Mester Stoorworm," she said, coming forward, "these others know not what they are saying."

The snake turned its head toward her. "No," it replied, "they are fools."

"Fools," agreed Twelve, and nearby Stout turned his back and muttered to himself.

"But, great Mester," the witch continued, "all of what they say is not untruth. Even fools can at times speak in prophecy."

"True," the snake said. "True."

"For surely you must have noticed, in your wisdom," said Twelve, "that the seas have been wild of late."

The snake raised its head and gazed about. "Yes," it said, "yes, I had thought that. I had thought that they were wild, and cold, of late."

"Wild, and cold, and treacherous," purred the witch. "Treacherous."

The snake turned its mad eyes on her. "The Mester Stoorworm," it replied grandly, "is not afraid of treacherous seas. The ocean holds no dangers for me."

"No," agreed the witch-brat, "naturally not, for the Mester of all stoorworms is large and great and can conquer the roughest seas. But there are others of your tribe who are not as fortunate."

"Others?"

"The other stoorworms are crying out for you, Mester. They have sent me to tell you that you are needed. They have begged me to go to you and ask for your help, for the seas are rough and cold and the stoorworms are being battered against the rocks. All of them, down to the smallest sea grub, have cried out for your strength to aid them in this time of trouble. Do you hear me, Mester?"

The forked tongue flicked in and out, and the thick body washed against the stone. "Yes," said the serpent, closing its glowing eyes. "I hear. I hear."

"Then listen well, Mester, for the lives of your tribe depend on it. They have sent me and my companions—these fools here—"

"Enough," snapped the dwarf.

"—to bring you back to them," said Twelve hastily. "Will you come with us, Mester? Will you come to the rescue of your tribe?"

The serpent squinted at her; then, rearing up, it searched the pond and the white sky with its useless eyes. "Will I go?" it rasped. "Will I go? Yes. I will go where I am needed. My tribe calls out for me."

"Your tribe calls out for you," echoed Twelve, and Nob and the elf, who had scooped up the pile of blankets from the ice, moved forward.

"They call out for me," whispered the serpent wistfully. "It has been a long, long time. . . ."

"A long time," said Twelve.

"But now I am needed!" cried the snake. It began to unwind hurriedly from around the rock. "I am needed!" It whipped around the stone, its head following its body, until at last it was stretched upon the ice, writhing. "Yes!" it said. "Take me to them!"

"*Now!*" cried Needle, and he and Nob pounced.

The other two helped wrap the blankets around the stoorworm's body. When they were finished, Needle stood back and surveyed their work. The serpent was firmly swathed in covers, with only its head and tail sticking out. The head was still talking to itself. "At last," the snake was saying in a dreamy voice, "at last they need me. It's been so long, so long. I am so glad."

"Stout," said the elf, "we'll have to do something about that tail. Can you crack the ice around it?"

"I think so," said the dwarf, and moving forward, he began to chop at the pond with his walking stick. When the tail was free, they spaced themselves along the serpent's body and, with much puffing and groaning, lifted it to their shoulders. Stretched out, the serpent was perhaps fifteen feet in length; its coils were four hand's lengths around, and it was heavy.

They edged slowly across the pond. When they reached the snowdrifts at the water's edge, Needle, who was in the front, paused to call back, "Are we all right then? Everyone?"

"Yes."

"Yes."

"Yes." And so they set off through the woods, the serpent talking rapidly and nonsensically to itself.

The creature was so long and heavy that they had to stop at frequent intervals to rest. By the time they arrived at the cottage they were exhausted and frozen through. The only one who seemed to be unaffected by the journey was the stoorworm, which let out a stream of cheerful observations as they shoved its great bulk through the door.

"Rough seas, these," it said mildly as it was lowered with a thump! to the floor, and Hopeless, who had leaped forward in greeting, backed off hastily, hair bristling. "Wild seas. Long journey. Where are the others?"

"Oh, shut up," said the dwarf, wearily, and the four of them collapsed into chairs. Hopeless stood, his jaw open, staring at the worm. The fire had burned down, and Needle rose to shuffle over and poke it up again. Stretched full length on the floor, the stoorworm hissed to itself, its tongue quivering rhythmically.

"I'm coming," it said happily. "I'll be there soon."

"What are we going to do with it?" asked the dwarf.

"We'll have to keep it here for a while," replied Needle. "There's no choice. We'll have to thaw it out and keep it here. Otherwise it will just try to go back to the pond."

"We're becoming a kind of orphanage," grumbled

Stout. He paused, embarrassed, as all eyes turned to Nob. "Well, well, never mind. Perhaps we should put it nearer the fire?"

"Yes," said Needle, but no one moved. At last the dog found his voice, and lowering his head, he growled.

The snake blinked, its third eyelid sliding into place. "What's that?" it asked vaguely. "A storm? Do I hear a storm coming?"

Hopeless growled again, then barked, and the serpent twisted to look up at the ceiling. "Dark skies," it murmured, "bad weather. Storm coming, no doubt. Thunder clouds above."

"Doesn't it have any idea where it is?" Nob asked Twelve in a low voice.

The girl shook her head. "It never does."

"Storm coming," said the serpent more strongly, and glared at them. "Storm coming! Must go—must go warn the others." It twisted around within the layers of blankets, but finding escape impossible, it murmured, "Be there soon," and stopped moving.

Hopeless came to sit at Twelve's feet, his head on her lap. The others sat where they were, crumpled with weariness, soaking up the heat. Finally the snake lifted its head off the floor, stared at the fire, and mumbled, "Warm in here . . ."

Stout lifted himself groaning to his feet.

"We'll have to do something about it," he muttered.

The others came over to help him, and they dragged the snake here and there on the floor until it was coiled in front of the hearth. Then they unwrapped the blankets and made them into an untidy bed. Through all this the stoorworm said nothing but submitted to the pushing and dragging quietly, a faraway look in its ruby-green eyes.

"Let's hope it doesn't get some idea into its head and try to crawl into the flames," Needle said.

The journey there and back had taken them all day. Darkness was falling. Needle, edging himself between the stoorworm and the fire, began to cook their dinner. Nob set the table, and Twelve put out a bowl of juicy scraps for Hopeless, a special meal, to comfort him; but the dog refused to leave her side, and she had to sit by the bowl and stroke his head and talk to him. As he ate, he stole worried glances at the snake, which now slept royally on its pile of blankets, the flamelight curious on its tiled body.

"He's looking at me accusingly," Twelve whispered to the boy. "He's blaming me for bringing the stoorworm back."

Nob glanced down at the small moth-eaten shape huddled against her knees. "Perhaps he'll get used to it," he said. "Didn't you ever bring the stoorworm here before?"

"Oh, no. We always took it to a nearby cave, lit a fire, and watched it thaw out. But the stoorworm's getting smaller and madder every year, and this time Needle was afraid it wouldn't stay in the cave by itself."

"It's getting smaller?"

"Oh, yes. I thought Needle told you. It used to be a sea serpent. It really *was* the biggest stoorworm, the father of them all. But it started to shrink, and its mind became confused, and finally it just let the ocean carry it off the mountain. When it came to the river, it swam upstream until it found that rock. It's been living there ever since."

"And—and it doesn't know what's happened?"

Twelve shook her head. "No," she said, and her hand stroked the dog's head quietly.

Nob looked over to where the stoorworm lay. The ice on its scales had melted, forming a large dark spot on the blankets. It was folded neatly around itself, its head near its tail, its body a mass of gleaming coils. It gazed drowsily into the fire, blinking, but otherwise it rested motionless.

"Dinnertime," said Needle, and they ate in silence.

After dinner they settled down to their evening's activities. In the corner Twelve played with Hopeless; Needle and Stout read, Stout smoking his pipe. Nob sat by the fire, his chin propped on his fist.

He often sat like this. The burning wood twisted and curled, forming fantastic shapes, castles and gloating faces, demons' heads and strange terrains, spires and valleys and unicorns. The boy sometimes thought of his aunt Lace and her throng of children, her hatchlings, as she called them. Nob wondered whether his aunt missed him. He thought not.

The fire swirled to form a spire of mountains, dropping into a great valley, through which an army marched with flags streaming in the burning wind. Nob gazed through half-closed eyes, dulled by the warmth. And so he let out a startled scream when he felt something slide smoothly across his knee.

There, drifting lazily in the air just inches from Nob's face, was the head of the stoorworm.

Behind the boy, Stout coughed and knocked his pipe against his chair as he and the elf glanced up from their books.

The snake leaned forward. "My sea," it said confidentially, "was very big and dark."

Nob did not know what to do. He stared at the creature in terror as it leaned even closer, its eyes gleaming red in the half-light of the flames.

Its thin flat tongue flared out inquisitively. "Dark," the stoorworm said, "and large. So large. It was my sea."

"Yes," the boy managed to say finally.

"Yes," the snake sighed. "Yes. And my mountain . . . that, too, was large, and jagged, with little spires. I remember those spires."

The snake's head was very close to his face. Nob

could see that the icicle which had hung from its chin had melted, leaving behind a few long hairs, which curved back stiffly from its jaw.

"In the summer," it whispered to him in its dry, raspy voice, "in the summer, oh, all the stoorworms would gather round my mountain . . . *my* mountain, you see, because I was the Mester Stoorworm. The Mester. And they would play there, and sing to me, and the sea would ripple with their bodies. They would sing to me . . . the wonderful old songs. And when I heard them, I would climb up on my mountain, and there I would stand and sing until my song reached the stars . . . the stars.

"And then," said the snake, desperate in its memories, "and then in the winter, in the winter, the ocean would grow cold and harsh, and the waves would wear white; and I would go to the uppermost peak of my mountain and curl around it, in the shelter of the trees, and sleep until the songs of the others awakened me . . . awakened me. I slept," it added firmly, "without dreams."

The snake stopped, its head held rigid, as if listening.

"Ssso you sssee," it hissed, "you sssee, I'll never let them take my mountain from me. Nnnnnever. Because if I did . . . if I went away from it . . . if I went away, you see, I would die.

"I would die," the creature repeated, and turning toward the flames, it gazed into them dully for a moment before letting its head slip down into Nob's lap.

"Warm in here . . ." it murmured.

Nob slowly lifted a hand and touched it on the head. He saw now that the stoorworm's back was covered with tiny bumps that looked as if they had once been part of a great spiny ridge. Its scales were mottled as if lichen and tiny sea animals still clung to them. Nob stroked the blunt head gently.

"*Aaaaaaaaaaahhhhhhhhhhh* . . ." sighed the creature, purring and twisting like a cat.

And there they rested, in the warmth of the flames, while behind them Stout and Needle sat stiffly in their chairs, their books lying open and forgotten on their laps.

F I V E

HE WINTER WAS HARSH THAT YEAR. IT lasted long and cold, and for many months the forest creatures hid within their caves and burrows. The naiads slept quietly on the riverbed. In the inmost chamber of her hill Granny Weil sat rubbing her hands over the fire, cooking up a variety of soups, and talking ceaselessly to her sleeping dog. Elsewhere in the forest the goblins and bogles snuggled into their messy leaf-lined burrows and rested. The dwarfs sat in their caves, deep in darkness lit only by a small fire, and smoked their pipes. And in the ramshackle cottage Needle and Stout and Twelve and Nob read and cooked and argued, venturing outside only to break the ice in the stream and melt it down for drinking water or to scratch the ground for roots to eat. Hopeless sat by the flames and shivered; he was getting old. Twelve sat by him most of the time, talking to him as Granny had talked to her dog, covering him with blankets and stroking his ratty hair. And Nob sat often by the Mester Stoorworm, which, once it had thawed out, decided to make its home around the legs of the table, where it curled up neatly. It made it harder to sit at the table for meals, but the stoorworm flatly refused to move. Stout had planted his chair over the creature's bulk on the second day, and the others had followed suit, so now when they sat and ate, the snake lay peacefully between the legs of their chairs. It let out a squawk when anyone forgot and tried to move backward.

A strange affection had sprung up between the stoorworm and the boy. The stoorworm still insisted that it was in the sea, wrapped around its great rock, but Nob was the only one in the cottage who would indulge it, and listen for hours to its memories, the wanderings of its poor lonely mind. The boy would sit by it and take its head upon his knee, where the snake would gaze abstractedly at him, purring as Nob rubbed the spines along its back. It would hiss, as if building up strength from within, gray steam escaping from its nostrils. Then it would open its red mouth and tell meandering tales of its former life. It had a memory long as its body, and when it spoke wistfully of sea grasses along the shore and the shape of coral under the moon, Nob could feel its yearning. And sometimes Nob would speak, in a low voice, about his aunt's home and the crowd of children and the one lonely boy in their midst. The snake would lean on his knee and hiss to itself as it listened. Its gaze was soft and confused, and Nob was never sure how much it understood. But it was a comfort for him to talk all the same.

And so the winter months wore on, and the snow slept outside their door. One day the one creature in all the forest who traveled in winter came to the cottage.

Twelve went to the door and threw it wide open. "Hello, Rasp!" she said, taking him by the arm and leading him in.

"Welcome!" said Stout, and "Welcome!" cried Needle, and even Hopeless shuffled forward from the hearth, his tail swaying. The stoorworm twisted about to get a better look, and Nob rose to his feet.

"Thank you all very much," said the stranger. He shook Needle's hand heartily, and Stout's, and turned to take off his cloak.

"Come here," said Twelve, and pulled him toward the table. "Sit down, sit down, there you are. What would you like to eat?"

"Whatever you have," he said.

She went over to the cooking pot and served him a bowl of groats, with a thick slice of bread, some butter and cheese, and a cup of smoking black tea. She put the food in front of him and seated herself at his side, her elbows sharp and eager against the table. "What news, Rasp? What news?"

The stranger smiled at her and at the others. His eyes rested briefly on Nob. Rasp was neither old nor young but had a pleasant weather-beaten face, cheerful and ravaged, with startling blue eyes and a thatch of soft brown hair, the shade of field mouse fur. He was dressed in rags. His tunic, his jacket, his cloak, his pants—all were worn and shredded, covered with burrs and mud and twigs. He had a wet smear of dirt across his cheek. He gazed at Nob, the ghost of a smile lingering on his face, and nodded.

"Why, you're the one with news," he remarked to Twelve. "The forest has been talking about nothing but the boy you found."

"Yes, well," said Twelve with a swift glance at Nob, "he's been here for a while now. He came with us to see Granny."

The stranger nodded. "So I heard." He turned to Nob. "And what exactly did you do, boy, to make her so afraid of you?"

Nob turned scarlet. "I—I told her a story."

Rasp looked at him with interest. "Is that so?" he asked; all at once he felt something under his chair begin to move, and he turned to find the stoorworm hanging in the air beside him.

A sudden smile appeared on Rasp's face. Lifting one hand to cup the snake's jaw, he said, "Greetings, stoorworm. Well met, again."

"Halt," began the stoorworm, confused. "Halt, you. Who goes there?"

"Why, Mester," said Rasp, "don't you recognize a friend?"

"The Mester Stoorworm has no friends, foolish one," it replied. "No friends. The Mester Stoorworm is great and powerful and has no need of friends. Why, it has only to open its mouth and breathe out, and its fiery breath would ravage the world. It has only to reach out with its great forked tongue to throw entire towns and mountains into the boiling sea. It has only—"

"Enough!" cried Stout. They had endured this speech several times a day ever since the snake had come to live with them. The stoorworm stopped, bewildered.

Rasp stroked its knobbly back and said, "True, true, the Mester has no friends; he is above all that. Think of me merely as your loyal subject, stoorworm."

The stoorworm, pacified, slid back beneath the table.

"Well, now, Rasp," said Needle, lacing his fingers together on the dark wood, "tell us everything. Tell us of your travels."

"The badgers say hello," Rasp replied, "and the prickly-hogs, the ones that live on the bank of the stream. I was visiting them when I heard about the stoorworm. I went to the pond right away, but the stoorworm wouldn't leave by itself, so I told Kay to go to you for help. The ravens came here then?"

"Yes, they did," snapped the dwarf.

Rasp laughed. "It's not easy," he said, "but then we can't just let him die."

The dwarf did not answer, but Twelve leaned forward and tugged at Rasp's sleeve. "Tell me," she said, "what do you have for me this time, Rasp?"

"Twelve!" said Needle.

"Now what in the world makes you think I've brought you something, you little terror?" Rasp said.

Twelve laughed. "Is it a wood carving?"

"Why, I brought you one of those three winters ago."

"A jar of herbs?"

"Don't you have enough herbs already, princess?"

"I know what it is! I know! It's a pet, isn't it?"

Rasp smiled down at her. "Now tell me, what use would you have for another pet, with Hopeless and the stoorworm here?"

Twelve glanced down at the snake, coiled beneath her chair. "I don't like the stoorworm, very much," she said in a low voice. "It's Nob's pet anyway."

"Is that so?" said Rasp, gazing at the boy thoughtfully. Twelve pulled at his sleeve again.

"All right, all right, I give up!" she said. "I give up!"

"Twelve, your manners," said Needle stiffly. Rasp grinned and dug into his pocket. His eyes widened in dismay.

"Oh, no," he said, and coughed, and checked his other pocket and his breast pocket, and searched in the cuffs of his pants, all the while muttering to himself. Twelve watched him, laughing. Every year he brought her a present, and every year he could not find it.

Finally he straightened up. "It seems," he said, "it seems . . . well, I've lost it. I'm sorry."

Twelve threw her arms around his neck, and when she pulled away, his face was shining, and he had his hand out. On his upturned palm rested a smooth round pebble, cloudy green.

Twelve stared at it. "A—a pebble?" she faltered.

"Look closer," said Rasp.

The witch took it from him. She fingered it and rubbed its smooth sides and held it up to the firelight. Then she gasped and set it down with an abrupt clink.

"Oh," she said. "Oh. I know what it is. It's a salamander stone, isn't it? Isn't it, Rasp?"

His smile answered her. She turned away and gazed once more at the pebble. Then she flung herself at him.

He laughed, hugging her. "It's not just from me," he said. "Someone else gave it to me."

"Who?"

"Who else would have such a thing?"

"Not—not Granny?"

Rasp nodded. "During my last visit all at once she started to grumble louder than usual and told me to finish my soup and leave. Then, while I hastily drank the rest of the bowl, she rooted in the dust and scraps and things she collects in the corner and tossed this over her back at me. When I asked what it was, she said I was an idiot. I asked if it was for me, and she stirred her caldron and finally she shook her head and muttered something about the little one, the little pretty one, the little witch. Before I left, she told me what the stone was—although she said you'd know— and what its uses are. She knows she doesn't have the power for it anymore, with the dog asleep and all. She said it was a healing stone. 'She'll probably just throw it away, or lose it' was how she put it; then she waved me off and told me she hoped she'd never see me again."

"A salamander stone," murmured Stout.

Needle took it up in his bony fingers and turned it around and around, saying, "I've heard of this before, but I've never been lucky enough to see one. A valuable present, Twelve."

The witch smiled. When Needle gave the stone back to her, she wrapped it up carefully in a piece of cloth and put it in her pocket.

"But you see, Twelve," Rasp continued, "I've brought you a gift from someone else, and for months now I've racked my brains for my own present to you. So here it is."

He reached inside his cloak and took out a single shining flower. The witch leaned forward, touching the blossom. It was white and silver, with small, delicate patterns of sea-purple etched on its petals. Its heart glowed pure gold. It was an earlypetal. "No!" she said. "Not at this time of year! How in the world did you find it?"

He gave it to her, with a bow. "The truth is that I stumbled over them by accident in a hollow near where the prickly-hogs live. The hogs had told me where they were, but even then I would have missed them and gone wandering off blindly into the forest if I hadn't tripped over a rock and landed right on them."

Suddenly, from underneath the table, a blunt head appeared. "You, there," it said. "Hail."

Rasp turned. "Hail, stoorworm."

"You, there," it blundered on. "Will—will you tell a story?"

"Certainly," said Rasp. "After my lunch."

The serpent glared at him. "You *are* the one who tells the stories?" it queried, its voice doubtful.

"Yes, I am the one."

"*Aaaaahhhhh.*" The creature nodded, and bobbing its head, it descended slowly below the edge of the table.

Rasp turned to meet the boy's gaze. "I am a droll-teller," he explained. "I told the stoorworm a droll once about itself, and it closed its eyes and breathed smoke through its nostrils and said nothing. Now I know that it was listening. By the way," he said, turning to the others, "what I've heard this year isn't good . . . not good at all."

"Yes," said Needle, "we know."

"I'm afraid," said Rasp, "that the naiads won't wake up this spring."

"Of course they will," Stout said, leaning forward. "Of course they will."

"The badgers had bad stories to tell me," Rasp went on. "Not so much a shortage of food, no real hardship, but rumors of infighting, and last spring a litter was born deformed, and—and other things. The same with the prickly-hogs and the rabbits and the wolves."

There was a silence.

"Well, that is nothing new," said Needle. "We've known that for a while."

They moved their chairs around the fire. The snake slithered forward to wrap itself around the legs of Nob's chair.

"The prickly-hogs were glad to see me," Rasp said, "and strangely enough, the goblins and bogles were, too. The change hasn't affected them as much, maybe because they had so little to begin with. They enjoyed my songs."

"Were they kind to you?" Needle asked absently.

"Well, as kind as goblins can be," said Rasp, laughing. "Sour milk for breakfast, dead mice for supper, that sort of thing. They think everyone likes what they like. I told them a few drolls and left."

Stout lowered his pipe, knocked it against the arm of the chair, and said, "Why not tell us a droll now, Rasp?"

Rasp looked up at the ceiling and smiled to himself. "All right," he said. "I'll tell you a droll about the trees."

"Oh, yes!" cried Twelve, coming over to sit on the floor next to him.

Rasp's voice was soft and pleasant, with a deep ring of enjoyment in it. *This is not much of a story*, Nob thought briefly. Then he did not think much else, for Rasp's words crowded into his mind. Rasp did not seem to be talking about anything in particular, but now and then, caught between many words, the boy could hear a snatch or two about roots and twigs and the sun, about water and moist clods of earth, about wood sap surging. As Rasp talked, Nob began to see the rain falling on branches, the endless movement within the bark, sap pouring, the drinking of light like water. He saw all these things, and more: leaves trembling before the stars; the heavy drowsiness of winter; dreams of spring and awakening; small animals in their nests; the mindless chatter of birds.

Nob sat, his head nodding, half in a dream, and when Rasp stopped, the boy felt a sharp pang. His mind cleared, and looking up, he saw the others awakening.

"Thank you," whispered the witch, curled up at Rasp's feet. "Thank you . . ."

"Thank you, Rasp."

"Thank you," said Needle and Stout, and sighing and stretching, they stood up and began to ready the table. The light was failing outside the house; when Needle opened the door, the cold wind beat on his face and rushed past him into the room.

"Dinner," the elf announced presently; and the bowls were set forth, and filled, and emptied, and filled again; and all was quiet, except for the sounds of eating and the whisperings of the fire and, outside, the low doleful notes of a nighthatch.

SIX

ASP STAYED ON WITH THEM AS THE WIN-
ter drew to an end. Early one morning,
when the snow was melting and the sun
burned cold and bright in a yellow sky,
he took up his walking stick.

"No more drolls?" asked the boy, running outside,
and Rasp leaned down, saying, "No more right now,
but when we meet each other again, I'll have new ones
to tell you." During his stay in the cottage he had told
three drolls: the first one about the trees; the second, a
few days later, about an herb called sage grass, a long
tale of each leaf and stem and root; and the last, at the
very end, about the goblins, a storm of ugly thoughts
and faces and thick, grating speech.

"You should practice your own stories," said Rasp,

frowning at him, "for when you go back to your people."

"I'm never going back," said Nob.

"Well, well," said Rasp, looking up at the sun, "we'll see."

"I'm not going!" cried the boy, and he turned and limped back inside.

Rasp hoisted his walking stick and smiled at Needle and Stout and Twelve. Then, without a word, he left them, striding into the shadowy corridor formed by the trees.

And so the winter waned, and the earlypetals grew thick and white on the grass. The forest yawned and roused itself, grumbling. Twelve went out and talked to the trees again. They nodded in greeting and sighed and spoke to her about their winter dreams.

"There was a wwwwiiiiinnnnnddddd," a young elm said to her eagerly. "A great wind, which blew between my branches, and in it voices were singing, singinnnnnnnggggggg . . . it was lovely, I wish you could have heard. . . ." And it tried to imitate the sound, and its branches crackled and whistled.

"That's nothing," whispered a nearby oak, black with moss. "Nothing. I dreamed that I was moving, moving through the forest, around and around, with the stars swiiiirrrlllliiinnngggg over my head . . . sssswwwiiirrlllliiiiinnnnggggg. And all the forest people were runnnnniinngg, and dancing, and the flames were burning . . . burnninngg. . . ."

Twelve sat and listened, as she did every spring, for sometimes the trees had beautiful dreams, and sometimes ugly ones, but all worth listening to.

Late one afternoon there was a knock on their door. Stout opened it, with a snort of surprise. "Why, it's Wolly!" he said. "Come to pay us a visit, have you?"

From outside the cottage there came a thin, high-pitched whine. "Good day," the voice said hurriedly. "Good morning, good day to you. Yes, how are you, how are you, I am fine, thank you very much. Good morning."

"Come in, Wolly," called Needle. "Come in! It's been a long time."

Stout stood aside, and the frail figure of a man edged its way inside the door. He stood there, wavering on the line of shadow between the day outside and the twilight inside, and continued to speak in a high trembling voice.

"Good day, good day," he said, bowing. "How are you, how are you, good to see you, thank you, very well. Very well. Nice weather, eh?"

"Come in, Wolly," said the dwarf, guiding him over to the table and helping him into a chair. The little man took off his cap, wringing it vigorously in his hands.

"Hello," he whimpered, "hello. How are you? Very fine, very well, thank you very much. Thank you."

"Would you like something to drink?" asked Twelve.

Wolly shook his head. "Ah, no," he said, "ah, no, thank you very much, little missy. Thank you. Don't have the time. No time, you see."

Then he gasped and started backward as the stoor-worm raised its head from under the table to inspect him.

"Halt," it began. "You there. Identify yourself."

"Oh, my," whimpered the old man. "Oh, my!"

"You there," said the snake. "Speak up, I say! What is your name? What is the password?"

The old man clutched his cap to him, and Stout cried, "Oh, leave him alone, you idiot!"

Nob ran forward and took the snake's head in his hands. It began again, "Halt! You there," before he lowered it gently to the floor.

"I'm sorry, Wolly," said Needle. "We took the stoor-worm in for the winter. Now, what is it?"

"Thank you," Wolly cried, "thank you kindly! I came—I came to tell you . . . it's the yunicorne!"

He stopped.

"The yunicorne?" prodded the dwarf. "Yes? Yes?"

"It's—it's the yunicorne—the yunicorne . . . he's—he's hurt and dying!" cried Wolly. He put his cap down on the table, lowered his head upon it, and burst into tears.

Hopeless rumbled from underneath the table.

"It's the yunicorne!" cried Wolly, raising his wrinkled face. "He—he was out wanderin' . . . and some hunters found him! They found him, and they shot him, full of arrows! He—he got an arrow—right *here*—right through his heart! Right through his heart!" He gestured feebly, scrabbling at his own chest. "And—and I was there, all the time, right behind him . . . but he didn't make a sound, no, not one sound, until it was over . . . !" He lowered his head, and the tears ran down his nose.

"I thought," said Needle slowly, "that arrows could not harm a yunicorne."

"Never before," Stout whispered.

"Oh, no," said Twelve, finally finding her voice. "Needle, no . . . not the *yunicorne!*"

"I was right there," Wolly cried, his heart beating in his voice, "but he never made a noise! Not a sound! Just a whoof! as he was falling, and then . . . nothing!"

Needle leaned forward and shook the bony shoulder. "Wolly," he said, "where is he? Where is he? We have to go to him."

The old man raised his head. "That's why I've come," he said, placing a withered hand, fragile as a winter leaf, on Needle's arm. "That's why . . . to take you and the little missy there with me"—he nodded to

Twelve—"'cause I know that you can help him . . . I know that you can cure him." His face lit up, and he scrambled to his feet, pushing the chair away.

"He's nearby," he cried, shuffling toward the door. "Here, follow me, he's not far. He's not far." He vanished out the door, leaving his ancient voice trailing behind him, like a ghost. "We're acoming!" they heard him cry faintly. "We're acoming, sweetheart! Don't you worry! Your Wolly'll take care of you, you know he will!"

"Stout, pack the medicines," Needle said. "Twelve, get ready to go. Bring whatever you think necessary. What in the world are we going to do with *him*?" he said, pointing to Nob.

Stout climbed down from his chair and began to stuff small bottles and jars into a bag. "Leave him behind," he said. "He doesn't belong there."

The boy looked up at the elf. "No," he said. "Please. Let me go with you."

"What are we going to do with the stoorworm then?" asked Needle. "Hopeless will have to stay behind to keep it out of trouble."

"No!" said Twelve, stamping her foot. "I need Hopeless with me."

"Let me talk to the stoorworm," the boy said. "I'll tell it to stay behind and guard the house for us."

"Hurry," was all the elf said.

Nob went over to the stoorworm. Kneeling down,

he took its head in his hands and spoke to it. The stoorworm gazed up at him. "Yes," they heard it say, its voice growing in strength. "Yes, I will stay behind and guard the door while you are away. You do well to trust me. I will challenge all those who come near this mountain. I swear it: I, the Mester Stoorworm."

The boy bowed his head and murmured a few more words. Then he stood up and went to fetch his jacket.

They hurried outside, shutting the door behind them, Nob calling a quick good-bye to the stoorworm, whose only answer was a prolonged hiss.

The trees had felt the waves of pain that radiated from the yunicorne's fall, and those that were close enough to see the hunt had conveyed to the rest what had happened. They had tried as best they could to lead the hunters astray. As the yunicorne fell, the forest surged around him like a great hand closing. He had been carried to a nearby cave, and a bed made for him out of grasses and heather.

In sight of the cave, Wolly ran forward with a glad cry and pushed his way through the crowd of forest creatures gathered there.

"We had to take him somewhere, you see," he cried. "We had to take him somewhere. I couldn't just leave him there . . . no, I couldn't. How are you, lovey?" he moaned, sinking down on his knees beside the yunicorne's bed. "How are you, sweetheart?"

The crowd made a path for Needle, Stout, and Twelve. Nob came up behind, panting, and had just a glimpse of the strange-looking faces around him before Twelve reached back and pulled him into the cave. He found himself standing in front of the yunicorne.

He was not in the least like the creature the boy had heard tales of from the time he was small. Aunt Lace had told him that unicorns still roamed the woods. Among the rhymers there had been a few old women who claimed to have seen a unicorn when they were young, and ballads were sung of the graceful unicorn, which lived among the trees and never grew old. A unicorn, the boy had been told, was as big as a horse, with cloven hooves, a lion's tail, and a goat's beard, all as white and pure as an old woman's hair. From the middle of its forehead sprang a single horn, which shimmered with its own light when the moon was full or when magic was being done. Unicorns were never sad or remorseful or weary, and nothing could touch them, not hunters' arrows, nor grief, nor the passage of years.

But the yunicorne was none of these things. He was the size of a horse; but he was a muddy gray-blue, and from his forehead sprouted a great brown horn, the color of dead leaves. The horn was etched in a spiral, around and around, ending in an upward curve. His feet were cloven, but thick and heavy, and his back and neck were covered with shaggy fur that bristled

out like porcupine quills. He had horse's ears, which
lay back against his head, but instead of a horse's
nose, he had a small, snuffly elephant's trunk, with a
tusk on either side and a scraggly beard underneath.
His tail was naked as a rat's, shredded at the end, with
a small knot in the middle. He lay on his side with his
head buried in the heather.

Needle knelt and motioned to Stout, who was hurriedly unpacking the bag. Twelve moved to the other
side of the bed and knelt there, facing Needle. Next to
the witch-brat crouched Hopeless, small and frowsy in
the twilight of the cave. The crowd streamed forward,
murmuring, their voices low and tuneless. Next to
Nob stood a goblinlike creature, as bent and stunted as
a crippled tree, with a gray complexion and bulging
eyes, pale and smooth as eggs. He was talking in a
hoarse voice to his neighbor, a black wolf. On the
other side, about waist-high to Nob, stood a dwarf. He
was conversing with what seemed to be a tall, slender
woman; but as Nob stared, the woman's features began to flow across her face, and her body suddenly
melted and ran like a rippling stream. The boy blinked,
and there was the woman again, her long emerald hair
coursing down her back like water weeds.

Over to one side stood Rasp, his eyes on Wolly.
The old man was crooning into the yunicorne's ear.
"There, there," the boy heard him say. "There, there,

my lovey, don't you worry, don't you worry. There, there, my dear."

The yunicorne was covered with blood. It ran from a wound in his chest and from smaller wounds all over his body. Now he moved one foreleg and lifted his head. "Wolly?" he questioned in a doubtful tone. "Wolly?"

The old man shivered from head to foot, like a dog. "Yes, sweetheart!" he cried. "Yes! Wolly's here!"

The yunicorne cocked his head. "Wolly?" he repeated in the same quiet tone. "Wolly? Why did you go away?"

"No, no!" cried Wolly. "No, darlin'! I'm here, just as I said I'd always be! Wolly's here!"

The beast sighed. His head drooped. "Wolly?" he repeated. Then he slowly put his head down again.

The old man lifted his face to the sky. "Ah, no!" he mourned. "Ah, no! Please let him hear! Please let him hear!"

"Enough," said Needle sharply. "Twelve, are you ready?"

The girl nodded.

"Stout, do you have the medicines?"

The dwarf grunted, his eyes on the vials and jars spread out on the floor at his side.

"Good. Hopeless?"

The dog merely looked at him, sadly, across the massive curve of the yunicorne's body.

"Hopeless is ready," said the witch-brat.

"All right," said Needle. He reached down and chose one of the jars. He opened it, muttered a few words, and scattered a fine white powder over the yunicorne's wounds. The crowd craned their necks forward. Selecting another bottle, Needle broke it open with a sharp blow against the cave floor and poured a dark liquid into a bowl.

"Stout," he said.

The dwarf lifted a sparkling vial, rounded in the middle and fluted at the ends. He uncapped it carefully and poured its contents into the bowl. Needle dipped a finger into the bowl and made a mark on the floor by the beast's head. He repeated this in a great circle around the yunicorne; then, leaning back, he mumbled a long passage. He paused once or twice, faltering.

"That's right," Nob heard the dwarf next to him say. "'Nilana sor yn estasia nil,' that's it."

On all sides of the boy, voices were murmuring, rising and falling with Needle's speech. Twelve had her head thrown back, her lips moving soundlessly. At the yunicorne's head Wolly crouched and whispered, his words following their own melody.

"Lisorelliananil," murmured the water-lady, her features flowing and changing with the syllables.

Next to Nob, the goblin chanted to himself in a raspy voice, bobbing up and down on his bandy legs.

All at once the chorus stopped.

"Nilana!" Needle cried, and the crowd and the trees swayed forward; but nothing happened. Wolly whimpered into the heather.

Needle sat back, his face empty. At Nob's side the goblin clucked nastily, and the wolf lowered its head with a snarl.

"Whatdidwewhatdidwedidweforget?" sighed the swirling voice of the water-woman. "Whatdidwedidwedidweforget?"

"Too long," said a voice from farther back. "It's been too long."

"Quiet!" snapped Stout, scrambling to his feet. "Be quiet!"

The elf's fingers played absently over the jars. He shook his head. "I need time," he said. "Time to think. Let Twelve and Hopeless try."

"I'm ready," said Twelve.

Reaching inside her cape, she brought out a small packet and unfolded it. Inside was a smoky round pebble, Rasp's winter gift. She placed one hand on Hopeless's head and held the pebble under his nose. The dog sniffed and lowered his head.

Nob blinked. On Twelve's hand there hopped a tiny bird, brilliantly colored, twittering in delight.

"Hopeless," Twelve said, "what in the world is *this*?"

The dog looked mournful. Twelve held it out to him again. They both gazed at the toylike creature, fluttering and singing. The bird cocked one jaunty eye at them and hopped about in careless circles. There was a sudden silence as its song was cut off. On Twelve's hand there writhed a small red snake, thin as a ribbon.

The witch held it up to her face. "This is not bad," she said, "but it's not quite right. Come now, Hopeless."

Behind him, Nob could hear someone muttering, "Twopenny magic. A carnival show."

"*Sssshhh*," warned other voices. On Twelve's hand there crawled a red spider, large as her palm.

"Almost," coaxed Twelve. "Almost. Come on, Hopeless. Come on." She spoke to him in a soft, pleading voice. The old dog stared wildly at the spider, which was waving two of its legs at him. Suddenly the insect swelled and exploded like a balloon.

In its place stood a bloodred lizard. Hopeless's fur stood out in prickles. The creature raised its tiny head and sizzled like flame. A whisper ran through the crowd.

"A salamander," said a voice behind Nob. "A fire-lizard, by God."

"A salamander," muttered other voices. "A *salamander . . .*"

Twelve placed the lizard on the yunicorne's fore-head. It curled its tail around the spiraled horn and began to speak. It shone brighter and brighter, until the cave was filled with a piercing light.

The boy felt a shiver growing inside him. "Ah, yes," he heard the goblin mutter. "Ah, yes . . . the magic, the magic . . . I had forgotten. . . ."

The water-woman had her arms out and was sway-ing back and forth, her eyes closed. *"Yeeeeessss,"* she sang, her voice eerie, the sound of the wind through the marsh reeds. *"Yeeeeessssss . . ."*

The boy glanced around him, suddenly frightened. The crowd was swaying and singing in harmony with the salamander. The yunicorne's eyes were open, and he had an odd expression on his face. He seemed to be trying to remember something.

The chanting went on and on. At last the yunicorne lifted his head, his tusks shining in the salamander's glow. With a grunt and a heave, he lurched to his feet. The crowd shouted its approval. The fire-lizard crawled up to the tip of the spiraled horn and crouched there. The yunicorne looked around, his knees almost buck-ling, his head low. The boy saw with dismay that the blood still ran down his chest and onto the floor.

Wolly saw it, too. "No!" he cried. "No! You'll kill him! *You'll kill him!"*

The yunicorne's head went up with a jerk. The sala-mander paused in its chant. Its light began to fade quickly, streaming away, dissolving into the darkness of the cave. The salamander faded with it, growing smaller, until it looked like a rose, then a coal, and then just a tiny burn mark. The beast's horn hit the ground, his thick legs folded, and the yunicorne collapsed, heavily, onto the cave floor.

S E V E N

T HEY LIFTED THE YUNICORNE AND BORE him through the forest. It was dusk, and the lights they carried shone faintly. The yunicorne made no sound as they moved. Wolly trudged beside the litter, his shoulders sagging.

They were taking the yunicorne to a secret place, a meadow where there had once been dancing and singing and great magic performed. The creatures of the wood no longer danced, and the magic was gone; but the meadow was still there, filled with mist, waiting. It was Needle who had suggested the move. "The cave is no good," he said. "This has to be done outside, under the sky."

When they reached the meadow, they settled the litter in the center and knelt around it as before. Then they began all over again. Needle scattered powders and muttered spells; Twelve and Hopeless sent a sparkle of lights showering down upon the yunicorne's body; Stout uncapped jars and applied salves. From time to time the yunicorne would open his eyes and look about wearily. Then he would give up and slide back into sleep.

Finally the elf sat back. "It's not working," he said.

"I just don't remember," Twelve said, nearly crying. "I can't remember. Even Hopeless has forgotten."

"All of us have," Needle said.

Wolly lifted his head. "No," he whispered. "You have to remember! You have to save him!"

"I'm sorry, Wolly," Needle said. "I just don't know how."

"No," said Wolly. "You've got—you've got to!" He stumbled to his feet. "You've . . . got . . . to," he said, pointing his finger at the crowd. "All . . . of . . . you! You've got to . . . *do something!*"

"Wolly . . ." Needle said, reaching out a hand.

"Go away!" cried Wolly, flinging up his arm. "Go away! All of you! What good—what good are you . . . if you can't save *him*? If he dies, it'll be because he was *too good* for you! He was too good to live here! Don't you see? Don't you see? He was *the only beautiful thing left in the forest!*"

The crowd surged forward angrily. Needle pushed Wolly aside and held up a hand. The creatures halted.

Twelve climbed to her feet. "Wolly," she said, "listen to me. What do you remember? You were a wizard once. What do *you* remember?"

Wolly raised his head to gaze at the stars. "Don't know," he muttered. "Don't know. Long time . . . long time ago."

The witch spoke to him as she would to her dog, coaxing him. "Come now, Wolly," she said. "Come now. You remember, don't you? You remember . . . how it was?"

"Don't," he said. He shook his head. "Don't . . . remember. Don't know anymore."

Twelve laughed, a sharp splinter of sound. "Don't you remember how you used to show me tricks? Rabbits into hats and hats into rabbits. You had a trick for everything, Wolly." She leaned closer. "Yes, you used to know," she said. "You used to know. And it's not all gone, Wolly. Not yet. Not yet. It hasn't all left you."

The wrinkled face stared at her, its eyes and nose and mouth a question mark in the torchlight.

"Rabbits," Wolly said at last.

Twelve glanced over at Needle. "Rabbits," she replied, nodding.

"Wizards . . ." he said.

Twelve grabbed him by the arms. *"Wizard!"* she cried. "You *were* one! So was your father and *his* father! Remember? Remember?"

Wolly staggered back. *"Wizard!"* he gasped, tears in his eyes.

He looked up at the stars. Slowly, slowly his eyes began to clear. "Fire," he said. "We'll need . . . fire."

At a sharp word from Needle the crowd scattered. One by one they reappeared, their arms filled with brushwood. They arranged it carefully in a circle around Wolly.

"Yes," said Wolly. "That's right." He raised one hand and pointed at the piles of wood. "Fire," he said.

The circle of brushwood exploded into flame.

A smile crept over the old man's face. "I *remember!*" he said. Stepping back, he plunged his hand into the flames.

There was a gasp from the crowd. Wolly lifted his hand, and they could see a fire-blossom, petals lifting, blazing in the center of his palm. He moved over to the yunicorne.

"Now, now, lovey," he whispered, "now, now, that's for you. Yes, sweetheart, it's for you."

The yunicorne could not lift his head, so Wolly leaned forward and placed the blossom near his horn, where the salamander had clung.

"That's right," they heard him say. "That's where it goes, doesn't it? Doesn't it? You'll feel better now, you'll see."

The beast craned his neck. His breath was shallow, his eyes fixed and distant. He could no longer see

Wolly or the ring of forestfolk or the trees beyond. Before him there danced a heart of fire, a cloud of soft flame. The cloud shifted and changed, forming now a group of petals, blood-bright, now an orb, smooth and polished, now a graceful figure, reaching toward him. The fire flowed from one shape into the next, now a salamander, which curled its tail and sang to him sweetly, now a fire-naiad, whose face flowed crimson and aquamarine, her eyes smiling at him through the blaze; and now the loving, wrinkled features of Wolly, who looked down at him as if from a great height.

The yunicorne stared up wildly. "Wolly," he said. "Wolly!" The old man's face turned and shifted and shrank to a glowing coal, which chanted in the voice of the fire-lizard. *"Wolly!"* cried the yunicorne in despair. The lizard laughed and slithered away from him into the darkness. "No!" the yunicorne cried out. *"No!"* He rolled over onto his stomach and struggled to get up. *"No!"* he cried, and with a pant and a heave, he was on his feet. "No!" he shouted. *"No! Wolly!"*

He tried to turn, but his feet were slow and heavy. His head dropped, and he began to fall.

Suddenly the fire-blossom spread its petals and surged around him, holding him upright. He stood, his eyes wide, trapped inside the globe of fire. Now, as the forest creatures watched, his features began to change. His trunk shriveled away, his eyes grew larger, his tusks vanished, his great misshapen bulk became smaller, daintier, his ears shrank into the shape of rose petals, his tail lost its ratlike nakedness and streamed with flowing hair, and the prickly fur that covered his neck and back melted away into the flame and left behind a mane of palest gold. And the horn, his great curved horn, sprang straight and true from his brow. The beast lifted its head and stretched out its fragile neck, and before their eyes there stood in the column of fire a real unicorn, its mane flowing, its horn shining crimson and gold. The unicorn reared up, striking out with its cloven hooves. The creatures shrank back. Wolly sat huddled on the ground, his eyes nearly popping out of his head.

All at once the globe shimmered and burst. The forest creatures shouted and ran for cover.

There was a long moment of silence.

They crept back, their eyes wide, to find the grass scorched and blackened in a ring. And there, in the center, stood the yunicorne, whole and well again, his prickly hair standing out along his back, looking around bewilderedly and calling in his soft voice, *"Wolly?"*

E I G H T

WEEK LATER THE STOORWORM LEFT. THEY had returned home late at night from the meadow, to be greeted at their door with a harsh *"Halt!* Who goes there?" followed by a vicious hiss. Stout had lost his temper and begun to swear at the confused snake, which was coiled just on the other side of the door.

"Fool! Idiot!" cried the dwarf, stomping around in front of the house. "How *dare* you! Move aside, and let us in!"

There was no answer. Then, after a moment, they could hear the stoorworm's voice coming faintly through the door. "What is the password?" it inquired stiffly.

"There *is* no password, you fool!" Stout shouted, slamming his fists against the door. "There *is* no password," he repeated in a whisper, and took his head into his hands.

"The password, please," insisted the dry voice.

Needle was holding the torch. He took up the dwarf's cane in his other hand and pounded on the door. "Stoorworm! Let us in!" he cried. "It's us, Twelve and Needle and Stout and Nob! We live here, Mester!"

They could hear the sound of scales rasping against the wooden floor. The snake's eye came into view through a gnarl hole in the door. It peered at them angrily.

"Tricks," it said shortly. "Lies. All lies. How easily do you think I may be taken in, mortals?" The eye vanished. "Never," they heard it saying to itself as it settled back down into position. "Don't let anyone in, that's what he said. That's what he said. My duty is to stand guard."

Needle turned to Nob. "Did you give the stoorworm a password?" he demanded.

"No! I—I said that we'd be back soon, and to stand guard until we returned . . . and not to let anyone else in."

"Is that all?"

"I—I think so," Nob faltered. "Oh, and I said that when we returned, we'd give the stoorworm our thanks . . . I thought it would like that—"

"I see," the elf said grimly, and going up to the door

again, he pounded on it and shouted, "Mester! Mester Stoorworm!"

The ruby-green eye appeared at the swirl hole again. It glared at them, distant and doubtful.

"The password?" it demanded.

"Mester Stoorworm," cried the elf, "I come to give you our thanks, our profound gratitude, for the service you have done us. You have guarded the door well and long. Now let us in, you idiot!"

The eye disappeared, and there was a hasty slithering behind the door. Then came the worm's voice, high and imperious. *"Enter!"* it called.

Needle pushed the door, and it opened. They went in to find the serpent coiled in the middle of the room, squinting at them in mixed gladness and fear.

"How did I do?" it demanded. "How did I do? Did I do well?"

"Very well," whispered Nob, glancing up at the others. "Very well, stoorworm. Come back with me under the table now."

"I held guard!" cried the snake. Nob guided it over to the chair and sat on the floor while it wrapped itself around the table. It listened eagerly to his words of praise. "I held guard!" it told him.

"Perhaps it will leave soon," Needle murmured to Stout, but the dwarf just shook his head and sat down heavily near the burned-out fire.

After the night in the meadow, Twelve and her dog began to go off into the forest by themselves for long stretches of time. The witch-brat would get up in the morning and rouse Hopeless, who awoke with difficulty, grumbling; then they would leave, and the others would not see them until midafternoon, when hunger drove them back. The elf would look after her, a puzzled expression on his face.

"She's getting ideas into her head," he said to Stout one morning. The dwarf was at the table, reading, his head enveloped in blue smoke. Nob sat by the fireplace, feeding bits of toast to the stoorworm.

"Oh, she's just a child," said the dwarf. He turned a page.

"Nonetheless, she's up to something."

"She remembers more than we do," replied Stout.

"More food, please," said a frigid voice. The stoorworm opened its jaws wide.

Nob looked down at the gray diamond head on his knee and dropped a piece of toast into its mouth.

The great snake arched its back and purred.

Several days later it left.

"Time to go," it said brightly one morning, and despite all Nob's pleadings, it did not hesitate. "Time to go!" the stoorworm repeated in a sprightly manner, and slithered eagerly through the open door.

It paused outside, its head up, checking this way

and that, in pretended fierceness. Its eye glowed blindly in the early sunlight. "Ah, yes," it hissed to itself, "ah, yes, let's see now . . . which way? . . . best, perhaps, to go *that* . . . no, no, no, perhaps I should . . . *hmmmmm* . . ." And it hummed and hissed, its blunt head darting about.

"Oh, stoorworm," cried the boy, "you don't even know the way back, do you?"

"What?" replied the creature, enraged. "Not know the way back to my mountain?" And it put its head down and peered about doubtfully. "How dare you question me, mortal?" it hissed, squinting into the trees. It had no idea which way to go.

Needle and Stout appeared beside them. "So, so, stoorworm, time to be going, eh?" said the elf jovially. "Do you need some help? The stream is that way," he said, pointing. "All you have to do is find it and follow it upstream until it widens out into your pond. I imagine your mountain has been waiting there for you all winter long."

"Of course it has," replied the snake, insulted. "Well, time to go!" it cried, and prepared to slither away.

Stout took it by its underjaw and turned it toward him. "Mester Stoorworm," he said, gazing deep into its startled eyes, "I have only one parting wish: that next winter, we will not have the pleasure of your company. Do you understand me?"

"Take care of yourself, stoorworm," added Needle, and the creature bobbed its head at him and at the dwarf.

"Thank you," it remembered to say; then it cried, "Farewell!" and dropped its head to the ground and wound its way in great gray curves through the grass. It was mumbling and hissing to itself as it went. First it slammed headlong into a tree; then, correcting itself, it crawled away into the underbrush. The boy watched it go. When it had vanished, he turned, without a word, and limped slowly back inside.

And so the spring deepened. The forest grew lush green, and the animals grew fat and content. There were fights among the bogles over food; there was a frenzy of nesting and twig collecting among the prickly-hogs and birds; there were tricks played by the ravens, mean tricks, pebbles dropped from above onto unsuspecting heads, food stolen, small animals terrified. Kay's troops had been sent out to find the rhymers and had reported nothing, out of spite: Kay knew that several rhymer bands were performing in towns near the forest. He cocked an onyx eye at Needle, chuckled to himself, and raised his wings in an elaborate shrug.

"No news," he said. "No news!" And with a shriek of laughter he was off.

And so the spring deepened into jade, and the bogles quarreled together in the grass.

Then the hunters came back.

It happened so quickly, one afternoon, that the forest had no time to prepare itself. The first news Needle had of it was a dark clot against the sky, heading full speed toward him. As it came closer, it broke up into a storm of ravens.

"Hunters!" screamed Kay hoarsely. "Hunters! Come quick, come quick!"

They hurtled past. Needle turned and ran into the cottage, shouting, "The hunters! Hurry! We've got to do something! We've got to stop them!"

"Oh, we should've known!" cried the dwarf. "We should've known! Of course, they'd come back! What fools we are!"

They caught up anything that could be used as a weapon—knives, the ax, Stout's walking stick—and ran from the room, Twelve and Nob trailing behind.

Needle looked around as he vanished into the trees. "No!" he cried, waving them back. "No! Stay there! Guard the house!"

Nob and Twelve looked at each other. The witch was wringing her hands. Her eyes were very large. "What will we do?" she whispered. "What will we do?"

"Come back inside," said Nob.

They went inside and closed the door and moved the table in front of it. Then they sat down and looked at each other. There was nothing to say. Far away they could hear shouts and whistlings in the trees. Dull as turtles, they sat and waited. Next to them, Hopeless scratched himself, grumbling in his sleep.

It seemed to the hunters that wherever they rode, the paths before them twisted and came to unexpected dead ends. They cursed, reined back their horses, and whirled about to charge off in another direction. Everywhere they turned they found their way blocked by undergrowth or logs or a massive elm or oak.

In the time of the forest's strength it had always been the hunters who had been cautious, but year by year the men had grown braver, venturing deeper into the woods. Now it was the forest that was afraid. The hunters knew they had shot a unicorn; but it had vanished as it fell, and they were determined to find another. They galloped here and there, using their arrows against anything that moved.

Before them, the forest creatures ran for their lives. The naiads disappeared beneath the surface of the stream and hung there, suspended, their hair like emeraldweed. The bogles came out of the ground and gestured angrily at the hunters, but when one of the men reined in his horse and turned back, crying,

"Whoa there! Whoa! Come on, there's something in those bushes!" the creatures took fright and shambled back hastily into their burrows and crouched there, trembling. They shut their eyes and prayed. Above them galloped the horses, the sound of their hooves thundering within the earth. Some of the bogles' ceilings caved in, burying them, and they suffocated in the dirt.

Granny Weil heard the shouting and the sound of hooves, and perhaps she even heard the silent prayers of the bogles; but she did nothing. She did not venture outside her cave. She sat at the heart of the snail's shell and stoked up the fire and mumbled to herself, making signs in the air with her hands. The old dog slept on the floor beside her.

The hunters frightened a rabbit from its hole and put an arrow through its throat.

They stampeded over a badger's burrow, knocking it in, and when the badger crept out, trembling, and tried to run, they rode over it and crushed it.

They chased after a fox, which, shaking and foaming, dodged through the trees, eluding them until it caught its leg in a hole. It watched them solemnly as they killed it.

They did not get near the yunicorne. Wolly had hidden him safely away in a cave.

It was getting late now. The shadows were creeping

over the grass. The hunters paused, gathering in a circle. It was time to leave the forest. Which way led out?

The sun drifted low, and the cold light came sliding through the trees. The hunters glanced around nervously.

It was then that Needle, Rasp, and Stout found them.

It had taken them hours, stumbling through the trees, gathering about them a group of dwarfs and goblins and wolves, before they caught up with the hunters. Needle was the first to attack. He went straight for the hunters, waving a kitchen knife in the air.

"I'll *kill* you!" he shouted. He had seen the rabbit killed. It had looked at him through the trees. "I'll *kill* you, all of you!"

The hunters glanced up. It was twilight, and all they could see through the mist was a tall, spidery figure advancing on them, its limbs flying out in all directions, a knife in its hand.

"I'll *kill* you!" Needle screamed.

The hunters paused, confused. Then they turned their horses and fled. Beneath the flying hooves were small scurrying creatures, with knives that pricked and sticks that beat against the horses' sides. The hunters shouted and spurred their mounts on.

They pounded through the trees, leaving their tormentors far behind. The paths no longer betrayed them but led them straight to the forest's edge, where the trees had formed an archway.

The hunter in the lead waved the others on. They thundered through the doorway made of leaves and branches and out of the forest, their cries fading in the gathering darkness.

NINE

HEN NEEDLE CAME HOME, AFTER MANY long hours of plodding through the forest and stumbling over his feet, he put his head down on the table and cried like a child.

Twelve and Nob stood near him helplessly. Stout explained in a few brief words what had happened; then he and Rasp helped their friend to bed and went off to sit outside, the dwarf's tobacco smoke lingering in pale question marks against the sky.

The next morning Stout opened the door to find a group of bogles in front of the cottage. There were about twenty or thirty of them. Each of them held a large stick and an ax. They blinked at the dwarf and, at a signal, lifted their weapons and honked.

The leader stepped forward. "Greetings," he said. "We come. We come to make battle, eh? Eh? When the hunters come back, we will kill them. We will beat them with our sticks. Eh? Eh?"

Needle nudged Stout, and Stout nudged Rasp.

"My friends," Rasp said, stepping forward, "my friends, it is truly said that the bogles are a great and valiant people. Many drolls have I sung about your quick hands and clever ways, yet I have not praised you enough. Accept our gratitude and the use of this humble abode—"

"*No,*" whispered Needle from behind.

"—and the surrounding lands," Rasp said hastily, "while we wait and prepare for battle. For it is truly said that hearts joined in battle sing the sweetest song and that those who live under the ground will fight bravely on top of it, and indeed—"

"*Enough,*" whispered Needle.

"Therefore, we thank you," concluded Rasp, "and welcome you here!"

The bogles croaked in delight.

"We have come!" the leader repeated. The assembly squatted down in the clearing to eat their lunch: half-gnawed bones, raw cabbage leaves, and a pungent drink made of ripe brackleberries.

It was late afternoon. The bogles had fallen asleep, sprawled over each other on the grass. The air turned purple as darkness fell. Soon a horde of twinklebugs and other insects were humming around the bogles' heads. The creatures stirred and slapped themselves and sat up, drugged with sleep. Seeing each other, they honked cheerful greetings. Then they got to their feet and began to think about dinner. There was a host of small bats tumbling through the air. The bogles grinned, and a few of them clambered up into the trees, where they waited for their prey. They crouched on the branches, unmoving; then, when one of the rag-winged creatures swept by, a thick hand would flash out . . . *and grab it in midair.* In all other respects the bogles were thick, slow, docile creatures, but in bat hunting, they were swift and merciless. They tossed their catch down to the waiting hands below. Soon the clearing was filled with the happy sounds of munching and bone cracking.

The bogles were also fair. They could have hunted down the bats to their home caves and destroyed thousands of them as they hung upside down in their midday stupor, but they never did, unless they were starving. They preferred the hunt and the grab in midflight to the dull practicalities of skimming their prey off cave ceilings, like cream. They chuckled to themselves in dark glee as they scooped their dinner out of the air.

Nob sat by the door, watching. All at once the trees began to whisper, passing a message back and forth in a flurry of leaves. The bogles turned to listen. The boy climbed to his feet.

"There's something coming!" called Rasp.

The bogles honked and abruptly scattered, fleeing over the grass. Nob could see a large shape blundering through the darkness.

As it drew closer, they could hear its voice. "Here we are," it said nervously. "Here we are, aren't we? Yes, indeed, sweetheart, we're almost here. Yes, we are."

Needle leaned forward and broke into laughter. "It's Wolly and the yunicorne!" he cried, and ran to meet them.

"It was Wolly's idea," the yunicorne was saying as the three of them came back. "He thought about it and then decided that we should come."

"Couldn't wait," Wolly chimed in, churning his cap. "What if they came back, and we didn't know what to do?"

Needle led them across the clearing, where Rasp and Nob joined them. At the door of the shack they all stopped. The yunicorne could not possibly fit inside.

"Just have to spend the night out here," said Wolly, glancing around anxiously. "We'll be fine, don't you worry. Don't you worry. **See?** We'll be all right."

"We could offer you a sleeping mat inside, Wolly," said Needle.

"Oh, no, no, thank you," said the old man. "No, I'll

stay out here with the yunicorne, no problem, no problem at all. Are we? No problem at all, you see, we'll stay right here."

"You could at least come in and have a cup of tea with us before going to bed," said Rasp.

This was met by a series of protests before the old man finally allowed himself to be coaxed inside. The yunicorne settled down beside the open door, in a pool of light, where it was soon ringed about by friendly bogles.

The yunicorne looked at them curiously, smiling to himself. "So you've come to fight?" he asked.

The bogles honked and raised their sticks.

"It's very brave of you," said the yunicorne.

The bogles looked at each other uncertainly.

"And you, eh, m'lord?" said the leader, squatting in front of the yunicorne's trunk, which sniffed about in the air, taking in the night scents and the odor of un- washed bogle.

"Oh, I'm not a fighter," he said. "Wolly thought we should try to do something if the hunters came back again. We're here to find out what that is."

There was an uncomfortable silence. Their questions had been exhausted.

"Did you have a good hunt tonight?" the yunicorne asked politely.

Relieved, the circle of bogles launched into an enthu- siastic account of that evening's hunt, which indeed had been more than satisfactory and had resulted in an absolutely stupefying dinner for everyone involved.

The yunicorne nodded, his ears pricked up.

Inside the shack Wolly and the others were sitting in a semicircle in front of the unlit fireplace.

"Let's try it now," Needle said.

"Let me start," said Twelve eagerly.

"Manners," replied Needle. "Manners, please, Twelve. Wolly will go first."

"Oh, no . . . " Wolly began. "Oh, really, I couldn't, no, I couldn't—"

"Come on, Wolly," Needle said. "You did it once in the meadow. You can do it again."

"No, really," Wolly pleaded. "I—I don't think I can . . . I don't remember. . . ."

"Wolly," said Rasp, "we're waiting."

The old man sighed and turned toward the logs in the fireplace. Not a wisp of flame answered his efforts.

After a moment he sat back, shaking his head. "No," he said. "I knew it. I knew it, didn't I? I said so. I said I couldn't."

Needle and Rasp glanced at each other. Rasp leaned forward, taking one of Wolly's blue-veined hands in his.

"Wolly," he said, "if I tell you a droll about the old days, about you and the yunicorne, would it help?"

"Oh, no," faltered Wolly. "Oh, no, please don't . . . !"

"Are you sure?"

Wolly nodded. "Please," he said, his voice wheez-ing, "please don't. I'll try again." Turning back to the fireplace, he furrowed his brows and stared at the logs.

Minutes passed. Finally, with a grunt, the old man sat back, and a tear dribbled down his cheek. He looked at Rasp. "I'm sorry," he said. "I can't. I just can't."

"Never mind, Wolly," Needle said. "You can try later if you want to. Stout?"

The dwarf put down his pipe and gazed off ab-sently. His people were good with fire and smoke, but Needle and Twelve had rarely seen Stout work a spell.

The dwarf lifted the pipe to his lips and puffed, twice. A blue smoke-flower floated from the bowl and drifted over his head. Stout beckoned to it, and the petals began to spread, one by one. The heart was dark gray. The blossom hung for a second before their eyes; then it turned into a puff of smoke that blew away through the door.

"Well?" Stout asked.

"Very nice," the elf said. "Very nice indeed. But we need something to scare them off, Stout. Don't you have anything a little more . . . frightening?"

The dwarf looked at his pipe doubtfully. Then he puffed, once, twice, three times, and a goblin crawled out of his pipe bowl, larger than life, with glowing red eyes and fingers that scratched against the air. The figure stood there, swaying, for a moment; then it turned, quick as a heartbeat, and sprang straight for Nob.

The boy screamed. The creature, claws reaching out, froze in midair and disappeared with a faint wail.

"I'm sorry," Stout said. "It's difficult to control sometimes."

"That was very good," Rasp said.

"Twelve?" said Needle. "It's your turn now."

The witch-child grinned. For a moment she looked startlingly like Granny Weil. "Watch this," she said.

She had one hand on the dog's head. Now, with her free hand, she rapidly traced some figures in the air.

Nothing happened. She frowned and tried again. She glanced down at Hopeless. "It's not very easy," she said. She patted the dog and crooned to him, "Come on, Hopeless. You can do it. We tried it just the other day, remember?"

Once again she sketched the shapes in the air. Then she shivered from head to toe. She and the dog shivered together, and the room went black as the candles blew out.

They could hear Twelve muttering.

"It's the old magic," Nob heard Stout whisper.

"Stop it, Twelve," Needle said suddenly. "You shouldn't be playing with this."

"Oh, shouldn't I?" cried the witch. "Shouldn't I? Just watch!" She laughed and snapped her fingers.

A spot of light appeared on the floor and began to grow.

"Oh, no!" cried Rasp. His chair scraped the floor as he pushed it backward.

"I knew it," Wolly said. "I knew it . . . didn't I? I knew what she would do. Should never have come here . . . never, never, *never!*"

"Twelve!" shouted Needle. But it was too late.

The light grew and flickered. Nob could see something dark in its center. Something dark, twisting, changing shape: first a dragon, small as a lizard, its mouth glowing like a coal; then a cat, larger, with yellow, slitted eyes; then a scorpion, larger still, the sting at the end of its tail bright red; then a lion. The lion turned away, and when it turned back, it had the head of a man, and its tail was gone. In its place was the long, segmented tail of the scorpion, with its gleaming sting.

Wolly moaned.

"No," he said feebly, trying to brush the sight away.

"Twelve . . ." said Needle. He tried to move, but he was fixed to his chair. "Twelve!"

"Don't move," commanded the witch. "All of you. The manticore speaks."

To each of them, it seemed as if the creature were talking to him alone. Nob heard it say, *"You belong nowhere . . . nowhere."*

The dwarf heard, over and over, as if in a child's rhyme, *"The quarrel with your people will never heal."*

Wolly, shriveled in his chair, heard, *"Alone . . . forever alone."*

"No!" he gasped, but the manticore just smiled and nodded.

Rasp, transfixed, heard it say, *"No words, no more words. Silence."* The droll-teller lowered his head.

Next to him, the elf sat stiff and unspeaking. He had heard nothing. The manticore just looked down on him, with strange, menacing eyes.

Twelve made a short motion with her hand and muttered a word.

The creature turned away. The circle that held it began to pale. It clung to the floor, dissolving into a spot, a pinprick of brightness. They watched it as it faded. Suddenly it was gone, and the candles burst into flame.

Needle lifted his head. "Never again," he said to Twelve. The witch shrank back in her chair. "Never again, do you hear?" And leaping forward, he slapped her.

Twelve clung to him. "What did I do?" she sobbed. "What did I do?"

"It was the old magic," Stout said to Needle. "Who would have believed she could do it?"

The elf looked down at the girl. His lips were thin and dry. *"Never again!"* he said.

T E N

HE NEXT MORNING, AFTER BREAKFAST, Twelve took herself off to sit beneath a silver birch tree at the edge of the clearing, Hopeless curled up at her side. The bogles honked at her, trying to start a conversation, but at the look in her eyes they backed away, frightened. She sat there all morning, her fist clenched in the dog's scraggly fur. Needle and Stout watched from the door.

"It's because of last night," said the dwarf. "She doesn't understand, Needle."

"She's still a child," Needle said. "I won't have her trying out every spell she gets her hands on."

He walked through the clearing, calling a greeting to Wolly and the yunicorne and scattering bogles before him left and right. The creatures tried to speak to him, eager for company. He ignored them, and made straight for the birch tree.

"Twelve," he said.

The witch did not look up. Her eyes were on Hopeless, slumbering on the grass. The girl's olive hair streamed all around her, and her face was closed: closed and locked, like a door.

The elf sat down. "Twelve," he said, "speak to me."

The witch stroked the dog's back.

"The ones who could have taught you are gone, Twelve. You have only Stout and me."

"I'm not going to stop," she said.

"Please, Twelve. Just the dangerous spells."

"Do you think I can *choose*? Do you think I can *decide* to remember just this or that?"

"You can choose which ones you do, Twelve."

"You think it's for me, don't you? You think I'm doing this, practicing my spells, just for myself. Well, you're wrong, all of you. None of you knows. None of you has guessed."

Her eyes rested on the still form next to her. Hopeless lay on his side, snoring. From the center of the clearing came the murmurs of the bogles and the dull snapping and crunching of day-old bones.

The elf looked at the dog; then he looked back at the witch-child, whose face was turned away, the long hair hiding it from view.

"It's for Hopeless," she said, in a low voice. "For

Hopeless! You're blind, all of you . . . you don't understand *anything*. Don't you see what's been happening? He's been sleeping more and more . . . at all times of the day and night . . . and I can't seem to stop it. Just like Granny Weil's dog. He explained it to me one afternoon, when I tried to wake him up. He said that as the days go by, he gets more and more tired. He can't help it, he says. So I thought if we practiced spells, just the two of us, he would start to remember with me, and then he would wake up, and it would be all right. It's—it's the only thing that seems to interest him. When he's not helping me with my spells, he drifts off to sleep. I can't let it happen!"

"I see," said the elf.

"And now you want me to stop! Well, what—what do you think that will do to *him*?"

"Twelve, I'm sorry. I didn't understand. Let me think about it for a while."

"Go and think," snarled the girl. "Go and think! Right now, I'm trying to remember how to summon a banshee."

That night they gathered around the table, and Needle tried out his magic.

He was afraid and only half-willing. He would get halfway through a spell, and stop, sighing, and shake his head.

"Just start with something simple," prompted the dwarf. "Can you do anything with smoke?"

"Call up something scary," urged Twelve. "C'mon, Needle, you can do it!"

"Oh, leave me alone," snapped the elf, and shielding his eyes with his hands, he sat for a moment. Then he began to speak.

His words were in a strange language. A mist began to form on the floor, taking the shape of a woman, ashen, with flowing hair and a long gray dress. Tall, terrifying, she smiled down on them. The room suddenly turned cold, colder than the fiercest winter, and it began to snow. By Twelve's side, Hopeless trembled miserably, his body half-buried in a snowdrift.

The woman turned to look down at Needle. *"Yes?"* she asked. Her voice was haughty and pure: the voice of a queen.

Needle stared up at her, his lips parted. The snow had formed a soft cap on his hair.

The woman tossed her head. *"Yes?"* she demanded again.

Stout, wheezing, shook Needle by the shoulder.

"Needle!" he whispered. "Needle!"

"I could kill you for this," announced the woman in her sweet voice.

"Needle!"

The elf blinked, and with an effort, he mumbled a few words through swollen lips.

"Have you disturbed me for nothing?" the woman demanded, but even as she spoke, her form began to disappear and was gone. The snow stopped.

The room was warm and dry as before.

"The sorceress Ribble," whispered Twelve.

"Beautiful," Needle murmured. "So beautiful!"

Rasp shook his head. He glanced over to where the elderly wizard was huddled in his chair. "Wolly?"

"Yes, well," Wolly said, "I've been trying all day, you know, the yunicorne and I, but no luck. No luck at all, you see. I'm sorry."

"No, Wolly," Rasp said. "Tonight you must try harder."

"But," he faltered, "I've been trying all day—"

"Just one more time. Come on, Wolly. Don't you want to protect the yunicorne when the hunters come back?"

"Oh, yes, yes!" Wolly cried. He turned toward the fireplace. Beads of sweat gathered on his forehead and rolled down his long nose. He sat back, breathing heavily.

"You see," he said, "there it is. There it is. It's just no good, I can't do it, not worth trying again. Is it bedtime yet?" he added hopefully.

"Wolly," Stout said, "we need you. I know you can do it if you try. Rasp?"

"I'm going to tell you a droll, Wolly," Rasp said.

"No," Wolly said. "No, please, please don't!"

"You wouldn't have it last night," Rasp said, "but tonight, if the yunicorne agrees, you're going to listen." Turning to the door, he called, "Can you hear us, yunicorne?"

"Yes," said the creature, his trunk curling in through the doorway.

"Do you think I should tell my droll or not?"

Silence. Then: "I must talk to Wolly," the yunicorne said.

The old man got to his feet and staggered out the door. There was a murmur of voices.

Wolly came back into the room and sat down in his chair. He gazed out of his faded blue eyes at Rasp.

"He says we should listen," he whispered.

"Very well," said Rasp. "Listen then!"

A wizard and his unicorn ran deep into the heart of a great wild forest, a jungle of trees and vines and bright, flickering birds. Above them the sun was hidden behind a ceiling of leaves and dark arching boughs, and all around them surged an ocean of flowers, many-colored, huge, with delicate glowing hearts and pale pink veins. The unicorn smiled as it ran, and beside it the wizard spoke a word, and the vines parted, and the warm green light shimmered like a lake on the path before them. They ran, and the animals watched them from behind the trees: strange, squat animals with flat bills and thick feet, needle-beaked birds with wild, clear songs, and dark, snuffly goblins, who stared out of wide yellow eyes as they passed. The unicorn's horn gleamed crimson and gold, and all about them the air was filled with puffballs of light, sparkles, and fire globes. They had been running for hours, but they were not tired. The magic swam all around them, urging them on. They ran, and the leaves closed behind them, and the animals gathered, small and shy and humble, to watch them pass.

Wolly listened, his head cocked to one side. At the door the yunicorne listened, his head resting just inside the room. Nob, his face open as a mirror, drank it all in. It was not Wolly, or even Wolly's father, or his grandfather, it had happened so long ago. But the truth of it sang in Wolly's blood.

By the door the miserable creature whose ancestors had once been unicorns put out a heavy foreleg and grunted.

The sound seemed to bring Wolly back. "Enough! *Enough!*" he cried.

Rasp stopped, startled.

Wolly turned toward the fireplace. With a motion of his hand and a low word the wood exploded into flame. The old man smiled, closing his eyes. The heat from the fire beat against their faces, and suddenly all around their heads were lights, air sparkles, blue, yellow, and green. Wolly laughed, a feeble dry sound.

"Go on, Rasp!" he commanded.

Rasp sat up, his hands trembling, but before he

could begin, another voice continued the droll. It was Nob's. His eyes were shut, and there was a smile on his face.

The wizard and the unicorn were standing in a glade in the moonlight. There was no movement anywhere. Suddenly, around them in a great circle appeared the forest creatures: naiad, goblin, elf, bogle, dwarf, wolf, hare, fox, badger, dog, prickly-hog, witch, cat, squirrel, and all the rest.

The wizard laughed, tossing back his head. The unicorn laughed, too, making a sound sweet and clear as water, and all the creatures joined in. They began to dance. Hopping, leaping, singing, they ran across the glade, circling the two figures that stood in the center. They danced all through the night hours, as the forest sang around them.

At dawn the creatures paused, looking up at the fading stars. They turned toward the wizard and bowed low, their heads on the ground for a long moment.

Without a sound they disappeared, leaving the two figures standing alone in the meadow.

The boy opened his eyes. The others had their heads bowed. Wolly clutched the arms of his chair. He raised a hand, and it was as if the walls of the shack had fallen away, and they found themselves in the middle of a meadow.

Twelve took Nob's hand and pulled him into a circle with Needle and the others. So they danced around the meadow. And in the center, the moonlight all around them, stood the wizard and the yunicorne. Their faces were lifted to the sky, and Wolly was laughing.

E L E V E N

HE NEXT MORNING RASP ASKED NOB TO come with him. They left the cottage, and Rasp led the boy over to one of the bogles. "Tell me what you see," he said.

Nob looked down. He closed his eyes. "I see—I see a passageway underground. Like Granny Weil's, but smaller. And worms . . . the worms are *singing*. They're singing to me. And . . . and caverns . . . big caverns with bats hanging from the roof . . . and we're drinking . . . sour milk. . . ." His eyes snapped open, and he made a face at Rasp. *"Ugh!"*

Rasp nodded. "Not bad. How about that tree over there?"

Rasp listened to Nob tell his stories all the rest of that morning. At noon, as the bogles were taking out their cabbage leaves for lunch, cracking their knuckles in anticipation, Rasp said, "That's enough for now." They walked back to the cottage door. "There's no doubt you have the gift. This is the best way to practice," Rasp said.

"I saw things when I was with my aunt," the boy said slowly, "but I never told anyone."

Rasp nodded. "Not many rhymers have second sight," he said. "You'll be a welcome addition when you go back."

The boy scowled.

During the next few days a group of dwarfs gathered outside the cottage along with some goblins and a few naiads, those who had chosen to wake up with the coming of spring. They came, like Wolly and the yunicorne, to find out what to do. The bogles greeted each new arrival with an ecstasy of honks, and Needle and Stout went out to welcome them. At twilight small cooking fires flared up, and soon the grass was littered with gnawed bones, breadcrusts, and small, tidy heaps of broken bat wings.

One evening Nob was sitting next to the door of the shack, listening to the naiads sing. He was leaning forward to catch the words when all at once he heard a low voice in his ear.

"You, there," it began uncertainly. "You. The password?"

"Stoorworm!"

"Greetings," the snake said. "Greetings, you there. How goes it? I left my mountain and came here."

"And how was it, there on your mountain?"

The snake shook its head. "Rough seas," it said sadly, settling down in a pile of coils at Nob's feet. "Rough seas. Haven't been able to find the others yet. It's spring, you know, and . . . and they should have come."

"I know," said the boy, stroking its tiles.

"But they haven't," said the snake, querulously, twisting to get its belly rubbed. "They haven't. I don't know . . . don't know where they could be. *Halt, you,*" it said suddenly, glaring up at a bogle to Nob's right. Rearing into the air, it leaned forward toward the terrified creature.

"You there!" Nob heard it hiss. "The password?"

The bogle croaked out an inarticulate answer.

"No, no," the serpent said impatiently. "No, that's wrong, you idiot. Try again!"

From then on the stoorworm followed Nob everywhere, slithering after him through the grass. Rasp tutored him each day. Nob sat near Twelve and Hopeless and listened to the low murmur of her spell weaving. He chopped firewood with the dwarfs and talked with them of ancient legends. One morning, sitting in the shade, he told the stoorworm a droll about its mountain and the sea and the sound of waves thundering against mossy rocks. The stoorworm hissed in delight and gazed at him, its eyes small and fond.

"No," it said irritably at one point. "No. They were *prickly* pines . . . prickly pines. They were on my mountain." And then, later: "That is right. The others would come and sing to me." And it hissed, yellow steam escaping, and listened, and smiled to itself.

Sometimes, as Nob helped Needle with the meals, the elf would smile and pat the boy vaguely on the head, like a dog. Needle was tormented. What if, by accident, they called up something horrible and then couldn't get rid of it? What if it got loose and hurt someone? What if it turned on them? He had tried out a few spells, cautiously, after the night he had summoned the sorceress Ribble. He practiced these spells diligently, day by day. *I must be sure to have these right when the hunters come back*, he thought.

Twelve had forgotten about the hunters. She had forgotten about everything but Hopeless and her new-found power. She sat under the birch tree, summoning dragons, griffins, snakes, and vultures. She and Hopeless levitated, shakily, off the ground. It seemed to her that this was what she had always wanted to do. She laughed all day long, her thin face glowing. She kept the bogles in an agony of suspense.

Rasp encouraged the bogles to try out their earth magic. They burrowed all through the clearing, leaving behind them long, scraggly rows of freshly turned earth. They built strange lopsided structures out of bat bones and left them standing, held up with just a word. Their abilities were not of much use, but they kept Rasp amused.

The trees had been posted as guards. "What better sentries than the trees themselves?" Needle had said. Now the ones on the forest border, the younger trees (for the oldest ones, the great, gnarled giants, lived in the center), peered about anxiously, their branches a caricature of alarmed hands. They saw nothing, through the long days and nights. They waited, and watched, murmuring to their neighbors, signals passing back and forth, but no one came. *"No news,"* they told Twelve, *"no news!"*

Every night Rasp and Needle and Stout and the dwarfs gathered around a small campfire and argued over their plans. Rasp felt they should converge on the hunters at once, herding them into a small circle.

"We must be sure that they go away and *don't come back,"* he said.

Stout thought it would be better to detour them first: let them gallop around the forest for a while, until they were tired and it was getting dark and they could be caught unawares.

"They'll be caught unawares in any case," Rasp pointed out.

Yes, replied another dwarf, but they would be more vulnerable if they had already had a bad hunt and were ready to leave. Then if, for instance, a manticore or a dragon were to appear . . .

So they sat and talked until late. The bogles were kept in a state of confusion. The elf did not want them involved; he felt it was too dangerous. "Look at what happened last time," he said. But the bogles replied that they wanted to fight; they had come to fight, and fight they would. They held their own councils, muttering and cracking bat bones in the darkness.

One day Needle and Rasp stood watching as Wolly practiced spells to change the yunicorne's shape. "We'll give them a unicorn, all right," Needle said grimly. "Wolly, what about those tusks?"

Wolly was sweating. He nodded and lifted his hand. The tusks vanished. The yunicorne raised his head.

"I *liked* my tusks," he said in a plaintive voice. "Well, well. Wolly, what are you doing to my feet?"

"Don't forget the tail either, Wolly," Needle said.

Nob had been told to gather roots and berries. "C'mon," he said to the stoorworm. They set off together, wandering lazily through the trees. It was a drowsy summer day, and Nob was half-asleep. A host of bees hummed in the bushes. The stoorworm looped behind him.

They doubled back on themselves from time to time,

never going very far from the clearing. Nob began to feel hungry. He stopped in a small meadow, sat down, and started to eat the berries he had picked.

"We'll go on after lunch," he told the stoorworm, which was standing guard.

Nob ate most of the fruit; then, with a sigh, he got to his feet and brushed himself off. All at once the trees began to sway and mumble.

"*Wwwwwhhhhhooooooooossssssshhhhhhh*," they said, and "*ooooooooohhhhhhhhh*" and "*wwwwwwwhhhhhhhhhhooooooooooo?????*" and bent as if a storm were rushing through. A few branches clattered to the ground.

Nob lifted his head, his hair ruffling in the sudden wind. "What is it?" he cried.

Faintly now, through the forest, there came a high silver tinkle, a cascade of falling notes. Nob and the snake stared at each other.

"Hark!" cried the snake. "What—what is it?"

"A horn," Nob said. "A hunting horn."

Now they could hear a drumming sound, growing louder, the dull thud of hooves against earth. Nob glanced quickly around him. "Come on, stoorworm! We have to get out of here!"

The snake's head was up. "The—the hunters?" it stammered. "The hunters are coming?"

"Yes! We have to get back to the others!"

The snake twisted around; then it dropped to the ground and curled away rapidly toward the sound of the horses. "I will challenge them!" it cried. "I will challenge them! How—how dare they enter the forest again!"

"*No!*" Nob shouted. "No! Come back!"

"Halt!" ordered the creature, rearing up. "Halt, you! What is the password? I say, you shall not pass! You shall not pass!"

"*Stoorworm!*" cried Nob, and running forward, he took its head in his hands. "Stoorworm," he said, "you have to go back! I'll stay and slow them down. You have to go back, do you hear? Tell Needle that—that I'll try to head the hunters away from him, toward the river."

"You—you will ask them the password?" it queried.

The horn sounded, nearby.

"Yes!" cried the boy.

"Very well," the snake said, and dropping to the ground, it moved quickly away. "No one shall pass unhindered!" it cried, and disappeared into the bushes.

Nob turned around. The drumming sound grew louder. A moment later the hunters, about thirty of them, broke through the trees.

Nob ran forward and grabbed the bridle of the first horse, which reared backward, nearly throwing him off his feet.

The hunters shouted to each other.

"The unicorn!" Nob cried. "The unicorn!"

There was a sudden dead silence.

"It was over that way!" Nob shouted. He pointed. "By the river! Come *on*, or you'll miss it!"

"What are you doing here, boy?" said the leader.

"I—I live near the forest with my aunt. Come on, we've got to hurry!"

The leader circled on his horse. He turned and conferred briefly with the other hunters. Then he galloped toward Nob. As he passed, he leaned down and swept the boy into the saddle in front of him.

"That way!" gasped Nob.

Half an hour later they broke free of the trees and found themselves on the banks of a river.

"Well?" snapped the leader, reining in his horse. "Well?"

"We'll have to cross," said Nob. "But it's too deep here."

The hunter grunted.

They galloped along the river, heading downstream. The reeds shivered as they went by. All at once the leader pulled up his horse. "No sign of it!" he said. "You're a liar, boy. You haven't seen a unicorn any more than we have."

A rough blow of his hand sent Nob sprawling to the ground.

"Back!" shouted the leader, turning his horse. "Back!"

Nob's head was pounding. He could hear the mur-

murs of the river, whispering to him in the voices of
the naiads.

He scrambled to his feet and pointed, yelling,
"Look!"

There, on the opposite side of the river, stood the
unicorn. It regarded them for a moment placidly; then,
with a toss of its head, it was off, racing with the cur-
rent, heading downstream. Its horn flashed crimson
and gold, like a star before it.

With a cry the hunters followed.

After several bends the river widened and became
shallow, with a pebbly bottom. The hunters threw
themselves off their horses and, slipping and scrambling down the bank, led the animals across, with loud
curses at their slowness. On the other side they
mounted again. Farther down the river the unicorn appeared, waiting between the trees. It turned and vanished into the forest.

Shouting to each other, they rushed after it. They
did not notice that the trees drew apart, clearing a path
for them. Nor did they notice that aside from their
own voices and the sounds of their horses' hooves, the
forest was still.

Nob stood where they had left him. He looked up
and down the river. Then he limped slowly after the
hunters. When he reached the ford, he climbed down
the bank and waded across. He tried to remember the
bits and pieces of Needle's plan. The trees whispered

to him, guiding him on. Turning, he plunged into the undergrowth.

Behind him, the whitewater currents of the river foamed and mumbled.

Suddenly, a little downstream from the fording place, a blunt diamond-shaped head popped up, gazing about like a nearsighted periscope. It paused, taking in its bearings, squinting this way and that; then, sinking slowly beneath the surface, it made its way upstream, its dark body forming a question mark in the water. Two naiads swam beside it, gesturing and speaking in gushes of clear blue bubbles. At the place where the hunters had crossed, the water-women paused, and the blunt head shot up again, squinting. Then, with elaborate stealth, the creature sank down again until its head just rested on the water. It traveled across until it bumped up against the shore. The snake crawled out into a clump of marsh grass and lay there for a moment before inching up the riverbank and moving away rapidly through the forest.

T W E L V E

HE UNICORN LED THE HUNTERS ON A wild chase that day. It ran in front of them, turning to stand for a moment in the center of a meadow, then leaping away into the underbrush. The hunters followed. Their faces were streaked with sweat, and their eyes were burning. The trees drew aside and watched as they passed.

The hunters pursued the unicorn all afternoon. Every time they thought they had lost it the creature would appear nearby. And each time they thought they were gaining on it, it would vanish and reappear far away, like a spot of moonlight on a hill. Wolly's spells did not work perfectly, and the unicorn's shape kept changing, sprouting tusks, waving a wrinkled trunk, flicking a ratty, knotted tail. But the hunters did not see. The yunicorne was slow and awkward, but to their eyes, he slid away like a drop of mercury. Wolly slipped through the forest behind him, a shadow within the shadows.

The men were being led, with many turns and detours, toward the meadow in the center of the forest where the yunicorne had been healed. Needle had again chosen this place because it was filled with memories of power. By this time there was only a sliver of moon, and so the magic would have to be done in near darkness. Needle cursed when he realized this and sat down in the grass. Twelve stood next to him, Hopeless crouched at her feet. Rasp was leaning on his cane nearby. They all jumped when Nob appeared at the edge of the clearing.

He came forward, and Needle nodded to him. "Good work," the elf said.

"The hunters?" asked Nob.

"They'll be here soon enough."

Nob sat down. No one spoke. Hopeless's eyes caught the last glimmer of sunset and burned red, briefly.

The hunters did not notice the creeping darkness. All they could see was the unicorn, fleeing before them, leading them on and on. The horses were wet, their sides heaving.

At last the hunters reached the meadow. They galloped toward it, their eyes fixed on the unicorn, which stood in the center. They charged into the meadow and stopped.

The unicorn had vanished.

Overhead the stars were coming out from behind the clouds. The hunters slid to the ground.

"Oh, God," moaned one of them, leaning against his horse. "How—how long has it been?"

"We've lost it," said another. "We've lost it!"

There was a sudden burst of light behind them, and they whirled about. There at the edge of the meadow stood the unicorn.

"Hunters," it said, *"why are you chasing me?"*

The men stood, stunned.

"Hunters," it continued, *"why do you want to kill me?"*

Needle and the others watched from behind the trees.

The unicorn moved forward, stopping before one of the horses. Then, with a swift motion, it bowed its neck and brushed the horse with its horn, and the horse cantered off into the night.

The unicorn went to each horse in turn, and on its touch each animal fled.

There was a movement next to Needle, and Wolly appeared. The old man's eyes swam with spells.

"Wolly," Needle whispered, "it's time. Let him go."

Wolly nodded. In the clearing the unicorn looked up.

The hunters still stood unmoving. The unicorn turned back to them and said, *"Do not come here again."* Then it was gone.

Needle turned to Twelve. The witch sat a little apart, one arm around Hopeless.

"Twelve," the elf said.

With a deep breath she buried her hands in Hopeless's fur. *"Now!"* she said.

In the clearing, where the unicorn had stood, there wavered a cloud of light. Twice it flickered and went out, and twice the witch closed her eyes and brought it back.

"Now," she whispered again, stretching out her hand.

And there, hideous-dark, stood the manticore. It bent a gentle face down on the hunters.

Needle gasped. "No!" he said in dismay. "Twelve, I told you! Not *that* one!"

The witch laughed. "It'll do the trick, won't it?" she replied. "They'll never come back *here* again!"

Rasp leaned forward and shook her roughly. "Little fool," he whispered, "try something else. Listen to Needle!"

In reply the witch snapped her fingers in his face.

In the clearing, the manticore had still not spoken a word. The hunters stood paralyzed before it.

"It's too much," said the elf. "It could kill them. *Twelve!"*

But the witch, spell-drunk, would not listen.

The monster smiled. As before, it spoke, and each hunter believed that its words were meant for him alone. To one man it spoke of his wife, to another of his craft, to a third of his careful long-hoarded hopes. To each it spoke of sickness and decay and loss. The men lowered their heads, defenseless, huddled in a small, humble circle there in the middle of the forest.

"Twelve," said Needle, "stop it!"

"Yes," she replied at last, and raised her hand.

The manticore paused. The light around it began to disappear. The creature shimmered, growing thin and stretched, like the surface of an old painting.

Suddenly there was a burst of shouting and crackling in the bushes behind the hunters. Stout and the other dwarfs exploded into the clearing, brandishing heavy sticks, followed by a group of goblins and bogles. They sprang upon the hunters with loud cries. The men scattered into the forest in confusion.

Twelve paused to watch, grinning spitefully. Her spell was left unfinished.

The dog lifted his head and howled at the moon.

And so the chase was on. The dwarfs rushed after the hunters, waving their weapons and shouting. The men were fast with fear, but they had to fight their way through the trees. Some stumbled upon their horses, grazing quietly near the clearing. They scrambled into the saddles and, with swift kicks, set off through the forest.

The bogles chuckled and, slipping up behind them, threw bones at the horses, making them shy and unseat their riders. The goblins pricked the horses' flanks with knives, making them rear, and clambered up into the trees, throwing pebbles and bones at the fleeing men, who screamed as they felt small, quick hands grasping at them from the branches. A few of the strongest bogles waited, crouched on swaying branches, for a rider to pass underneath; then they reached down and swept the man backward off his horse.

One hunter, more resourceful than the rest, reined up his horse and circled slowly. He saw the small, bent figures, slipping through the shadows, some of them climbing up into the trees. He reached back, taking an arrow from his quiver and lightly notched his bow. Then he waited, leaning forward on the saddle, looking for a likely target.

Suddenly a dry voice spoke out of the air near his left ear.

"Halt," it said. "You there. You."

There, hanging in midair, its body coiled around a thick branch, was the stoorworm. It eyes glowed like jewels, and its fanged mouth was open.

"You there," it said, the long bristle on its jaw

quivering as it swayed back and forth, "did you hear me?"

The man opened his mouth in a dull squawk.

The snake glared at him. *"Idiot,"* it said fiercely, and opening its mouth in a slow, deliberate yawn, it sprang forward.

The man screamed. Reining back his horse, he turned and fled, sobbing and cursing.

The stoorworm slithered back up into the foliage and set off in search of another victim.

The forest people pursued the hunters through most of that night. The dwarfs drew the night mist together to form horrible shapes, leering faces that sprang out of the darkness in front of the hunters. Above them, in the trees, the bogles chuckled and built lopsided castles out of twigs and leaves. The hunters staggered here and there, shouting, but the only answer was the laughter of the bogles, and the hiss of the stoorworm, hanging from a high branch.

A few hours before dawn the hunting party found themselves at the edge of the forest. Their horses were gone. They looked like ghosts when they crept from the trees and gathered together in a forlorn group. Their clothing was torn, and their hair full of brambles. They stared and mumbled and embraced each other. They stood for a while, looking about, gazing up wildly at the moon. At last they set off in a scraggly group, back where they had come from, only the morning before.

Needle sat alone in the clearing. In the distance he could hear the dwarfs calling to each other. In front of him the meadow lay quiet, as if waiting. Needle watched it idly, his thoughts far away.

All at once there was a brightening in the trees on the opposite side of the clearing, and the manticore glided forward.

"Needle," it said.

The elf could feel his skin prickling.

The manticore waited. "Needle," it repeated.

The elf stood up slowly and walked into the field. He stopped a few paces away from the creature.

Behind them, in the trees, Nob appeared, gasping, dizzy with tales. He started forward to tell Needle; then he saw the manticore and stopped.

"Needle," he heard the manticore say, its tail writhing in the grass, the tip poison-bright, "Needle, your magic is gone. You are brittle-dry as a husk. You are hollow."

The creature bent forward, bringing its head closer to the elf. Its tail arched up behind it.

"Needle," it whispered, its voice echoing between two worlds, "I am going to kill you. It is better to die than to live as you are."

Needle listened, his face sad and quiet.

"Yes," said the manticore, "I will kill you. I will take you back with me."

And it moved forward, drifting above the grass, one heavy lion's paw, claws extended, reaching out. Its tail curved toward Needle eagerly.

Needle waited. What the manticore had said was true. His magic was gone.

He looked down, and the sting was on his arm. With a sudden scream, he pulled away.

The manticore paused. "You have no magic left, Needle," it said urgently. "No magic. Come with me. I will take you to lands you have never seen."

The sting quivered forward again. Needle backed away, his eyes on that sad, loving face, crowned in its golden mane.

"No," he gasped. *"No!"*

The manticore came after him, swiftly.

"No!" cried the elf, and raising one hand, he gestured in the air. From nowhere words began to come to him.

"Li elanal li elor," he said, the sounds coming slowly, painfully. *"Li elanal . . ."*

The manticore stopped. Then it shook itself and came forward. "Let me kill you," it said sweetly.

"No!" cried Needle, and now, suddenly, the words burst forth.

"Li elanal li elor si emelor i noar! I noar i lo nior. . . ."

The monster stopped, looking at him gravely. Needle stood, trembling, crying out the spell. The manticore sighed and cocked its head.

"Si emelor lo anamor i guidor . . ." sobbed the elf. *"I nior leda!"*

Nob watched, clinging to the tree like a frog. The monster laughed, a horrible, shattering sound; then it turned away and drifted into the meadow mist. It grew smaller and smaller, still laughing, the sound becoming thinner and thinner, tinkling like a cat's bell. Then it was gone.

THIRTEEN

LL THE NEXT DAY AND NIGHT THE FOREST people gathered in the meadow, lit great fires, and drank and ate and sang. Rasp sat to one side, ringed in by eager listeners, and told drolls of the night hunt. The bogles and goblins sang to the dry whistling sound of bone pipes. Nob was telling a droll to Twelve, who sat next to him, her fingers curled in Hopeless's fur. The stoorworm lay nearby, gathered into a neat coil. Stout and his people sat and smoked, told stories and laughed. At times the smoke from their pipes would form an image to accompany a story being told: a ripple of mountains, far in the distance, as one of the dwarfs told the legend of Nord and the Jagged Isle; or a sedate cottage, smoke bubbling from the chimney, as Stout spoke of the witch Liu.

Wolly and the yunicorne stood together. The yunicorne was himself again. Wolly was mumbling, his forehead knotted, a look of concentration on his face: He was creating puffballs of light that exploded in mid-air, sending the prickly-hogs scurrying.

Only Needle stood off to one side, by himself, silent and pale, his face bruised with the memory of the manticore. He could still hear the sound of the monster's laughter as it faded away into nothingness.

Rasp came up to him. "Granny," the droll-teller said. "Granny Weil. We should go tell her what's happened."

Needle nodded and went to fetch the others. Nob and Twelve came eagerly, leaving the stoorworm squinting at them from the grass, and Hopeless, crouched on the ground like a small bristly haystack. Stout grumbled but came along, leaving the circle of dwarfs looking after him.

When they reached the cave, they lit torches and strode in, Needle in the lead.

"Granny!" he cried. "Granny! We've come to visit!"

There was no reply.

They hurried on, boring into the hill like worms. The firelight wavered weirdly all around them.

"Granny!" Rasp shouted as they drew closer. "Granny, it's us!"

His words echoed and reechoed, but there was no

answer. No familiar tremolo, creaky with age and disappointment, reached them from the center of the hill.

They went around and around until their heads spun. At last the corridor ran straight, and they could see the small room at the end. With a cry the elf sprang forward.

He paused on the threshold. *"Granny,"* he said.

They gathered around him, their eyes shining out of the night like omens.

The room was empty. It had a gray, dry, crumbly look to it, like a shroud or an empty insect case. By the streaming light of their torches, they could see that the ashes in the fireplace were cold. The cooking pot was in its place, squatting defiantly on the hearth, and the rows and rows of jars and vials and bottles stood where they had always stood, on the broken-down shelves, crowded together in dusty comfort. Everything was just as it had always been, except that Granny and her dog were not there. The room lay heavy with dust, filled with the fine, thin whispers of spiders weaving legends.

Needle sagged back from the door. *"Granny,"* he whispered.

When witches die, they do not keep their form even for a while, as humans do. When they die and their power leaves them, they crumble into dust all at once, within the space of one thought and the next.

Stout raised his torch, and there, beneath the sagging table, were the thin curving bones of the rat-dog. He had crept there and huddled in a small circle, to die. The spiders were already busy at work, spinning webs in the hollow spaces between the bones.

Twelve pushed her way forward. She stood in the doorway, staring at the heap of dog bones, her eyes huge and empty.

Needle looked around him. The others did the same. Then they followed Needle along the corridor, leaving behind the spiders and the dust and the crumbling white bones.

Once out, they filled up the mouth of the cave with rocks and dirt. When they were done, they stood there for a while before they straggled slowly down the hill.

The celebration was still going on in the meadow when they returned. Nob found the stoorworm waiting for him just where he had left it.

"Greetings," it said, and arched up to hang by his shoulder as he sat down on the grass. "Greetings, you there. A droll?"

"No, stoorworm. Not now."

"A—a droll?" it blundered on. "A droll, perhaps . . . of my mountain?"

Nob sighed. He leaned back and began a tale of a mountain in winter, with the waves crashing green and white against its sides, and the sea grubs riding high upon the crests like foam. The stoorworm listened, its eyes closed.

"You've got to be more careful," Nob said. "You mustn't freeze this winter. You'll have to leave your pond when the weather gets cold."

The snake swayed, meditatively, at his ear. "No," it said doubtfully. "No."

"Listen to me. You've got to leave your stream. Otherwise you'll freeze, stoorworm . . . don't you remember?"

"I, freeze?" exclaimed the creature. "What? I, the Mester Stoorworm, freeze to death? No, no, mortal one . . . the sea does not freeze. On my mountain I will be safe."

Nob sighed. The snake coiled back and forth, its eyes shut, the whiskers on its lower jaw bristling. It opened its eyes and glanced around, hurriedly. Leaning forward so that its tongue flickered softly at the boy's ear, it said in a loud whisper, "I'm leaving, you know . . . going away. Going to find the others."

"What?"

"Hussssshhhhh! I've decided. Time to go. Go find the others . . . the other stoorworms. They're waiting for me, you know."

"But, stoorworm . . . where are you going?" asked the boy. "How will you find them?"

"Hsssssss," it said doubtfully. "Why do you ques-

tion me, mortal? I have said I will find them: I, the Mester Stoorworm. My people await me. Even now they ring round my mountain, far out to sea. Even now they are singing the old songs, awaiting my return. I can hear them: I, the Mester. Do you doubt this, mortal? I tell you, it is true. It is past time for me to go."

"But—but, stoorworm," Nob faltered, "in spring you couldn't even find the way back to your stream!"

The snake reared up furiously. "What?" it demanded. "Not know the way back to my mountain?" It peered at him blindly, angrily. Then it swung its head around to glance back at the others.

"I've discovered," it hissed, "that if I swim downstream—*downstream*, mind you—my river empties out into the sea. The naiads told me. It's true, isn't it?"

The boy nodded.

"Yes," whispered the snake, its eyes all alight. "And then, once I'm out to sea, I will follow the currents, south, to my mountain. All I have to do is listen. The song of the others will lead me there.

"Good-bye!" it said. It dropped down and slithered away through the grass.

"Good-bye!" cried the boy, reaching out after it. "Good luck, stoorworm!"

There was a muffled hiss as the snake banged head-long into a tree stump. Then, correcting its course, it vanished in long S curves into the forest.

F O U R T E E N

HE RHYMERS HAD SPENT THE SPRING, AND
now the beginning of summer, wandering from town to town near the forest's
edge, playing instruments, performing
shows, telling fortunes from a line on the palm or a
bump on the head. Kay had kept a strict watch over
them. It delighted him that he knew where they were,
and Needle did not. Needle still asked him, now and
then, whether he had seen the rhymer troupes, but the
bird just chuckled and said no, with a shake of his
head and a ruffle of his dark feathers.

So it had almost been forgotten . . . until the morning when Kay landed in the clearing, with his people,
all shrieking Needle's name.

The elf came running. "What is it, Kay? The hunters? They haven't come back, have they?"

The great bird hopped about on the ground. "No hunters," said Kay, shaking his head. "No hunters!"

"What is it then?"

Kay smiled to himself. "Rhymers!" he croaked triumphantly, squinting into the sun. "Rhymers! In the town Rinaldan, heading south! We saw them there yesterday! Better hurry, better hurry!"

The bird cackled, his smooth eye bright with satisfaction. He had decided, at last, to tell the truth, knowing that the rhymers were about to leave.

"Rhymers!" he repeated hoarsely, and peered up at Nob, who had come out of the shack. "Rhymers! Better hurry, hurry, Needle! No time to waste!" Then he screeched, and with a flip of his wings he was off, a dark mote in the sun-streaked sky.

"No!" said Nob. "I won't go." He began to back away.

"You have to," said the elf. "It'll be another year otherwise . . . Nob!"

"I won't go!" shouted the boy, and he sprinted across the clearing. He disappeared into the bushes, his voice floating behind him. "I *won't!*"

He came back at dusk. He sidled into the cottage and sat down at the table. Needle glanced up and then stood and served him from the pot. Twelve, Stout, and Rasp looked at him but said nothing.

The windows were open, and a cool breeze blew in.

Needle shook his head as he glanced into the cooking pot.

"There's not a scrap left to eat," he said. "We'll have to go out to gather food tomorrow."

The next morning Needle woke them up early. He bustled around the room like a nervous hen.

"Come on, come on, no time to waste," he said. The others roused themselves, grumbling, and set out after him.

He and Rasp walked in front, talking in low voices. They stopped now and then to dig for roots or to pick fruit from a heavy-hanging tree. Stout strode along, humming to himself. Twelve and Nob lagged behind, laughing, Hopeless at their side.

"Hurry up, don't get lost, come on," Needle shouted from up ahead. He and Rasp stopped less and less, and the elf kept coming back to urge on the children. By midday they found themselves near the edge of the forest, where they stopped for lunch.

They spread out a cloth and sat down on the warm grass.

All at once there was a faint rumbling sound. Needle and Rasp glanced at each other. "Follow me," Needle said. "Keep low."

About ten yards away the trees ended and the road stretched out in front of them. They peered through the bushes, but nothing was in sight. The road lay empty, shimmering in the hot sun.

They could hear voices. The rumbling grew louder. From around a curve in the road came a large caravan of people.

It looked like a parade. At first there were three horse-drawn wagons in a line, with people running alongside. Then there came four horses drawing a large platform, a stage on wheels. On the stage were people dressed in brilliant costumes, scarlet and gold and blue. Walking next to the stage were more people, also dressed gorgeously, in crimson silk and yellow satin. They sang and danced, the children running back and forth, turning cartwheels in the dust.

It was the rhymers. Nob leaned forward. Behind the stage was another line of small wagons, on which each family had piled its belongings. The children were shouting and laughing. Their elders fanned themselves, lifting their heads for any sign of a breeze.

"Aunt Lace," Nob whispered.

She was walking next to her wagon, Gertrude in her arms, two small children pulling at her skirts. She looked older than he remembered her. She put Gertrude on her hip and, laughing, reached down to scold one of the others.

Now the platform rumbled slowly by. On it was a group of actors practicing their lines for the next performance. One of them, a young girl, stood in center stage, the others grouped around her.

"Laren," Nob muttered. He parted the bushes in front of him with his hands. *"Laren!"*

She had become a performer. Nob could see her twin brother, Lar, sitting at the edge of the platform, his feet dangling. He was tuning his violin.

Nob watched them, his eyes burning, as the stage rolled by and out of sight. He watched as the line of wagons followed it, vanishing around the curve in the road. He watched until the last rhymer disappeared in a cloud of dust. Then he sat back.

The others turned to look at him. Faintly, down the road, they could still hear the squeaking of the wheels and the voices of the children.

Nob looked up at Needle. "You knew they would come this way," he said.

The elf nodded.

"No one's forcing you to go, Nob," Rasp said. "We just thought we would give you a choice."

Twelve said nothing but watched the boy out of large dark eyes.

"Sometimes," said Needle, "I wish I had gone . . . when the others left. Stay with your own people, if you can."

Nob leaned forward. There was no sign of the

rhymer caravan except a cloud of dust, far down the road.

"Can I ever come back?" he whispered.

There was a pause.

"If you can find us," Stout said.

Nob nodded. He got to his feet and limped out onto the road. He turned to look at them.

"Good-bye," he said.

The forest creatures watched as he walked down the road after the rhymers. His pace quickened, and by the time he reached the curve he was running.